almost a hero

Other Books for Young Readers by John Neufeld:

Edgar Allan

Lisa, Bright and Dark

Touching ("Twink")

Sleep Two, Three, Four!

Freddy's Book

For All the Wrong Reasons

Sunday Father

A Small Civil War

Sharelle

almost a hero

JOHN NEUFELD

atheneum books for young readers

Atheneum Books for Young Readers
An imprint of Simon & Schuster Children's Publishing Division
1230 Avenue of the Americas
New York, New York 10020

Book design by Angela Carlino
The text of this book is set in Perpetua

Printed in the United States of America

10 9 8 7 6 5 4 3 2 1

Library of Congress Cataloging-in-Publication Data

Neufeld, John.
Almost a hero / by John Neufeld.—1st ed.
p. cm.
Summary: Twelve-year-old Ben Derby spends his spring break
volunteering at a Santa Barbara day care center for homeless children.
ISBN 0-689-31971-1
[1. Child abuse–Fiction. 2. Homeless persons–Fiction. 3. Death–Fiction. 4. Santa Barbara
(Calif.)–Fiction.] I. Title.
PZ7.N4425A1 1995
[Fic]–dc20

Acknowledgments

My deep gratitude to Bronya and Andy Galef, who so generously deposited me on my editor's doorstep; to Jonathan Lanman, that editor, who invested time and effort with a vision others hadn't; to Patricia Buckley, for her wise counsel; to Ann and Mal Barasch, for their hospitality and friendship; to Winston Foote, for his ever-cheerful encouragement.

Most especially, to Patricia Nixon in Santa Barbara for allowing me to visit "Sidewalk's End" and, best of all, to work there, and who passed me from source to source, people of infinite goodwill and patience all.

*F*or Joanna Barnes Warner,
who led me to the treasure

chapter one

My first funeral. My dad sits next to me. I'm trying to figure out what I should be feeling. There is something in the back of my mind that's moving, sneaking up on me. For some reason, I feel almost afraid of whatever it will be.

Ten o'clock on a Saturday morning, the church is jammed with people who couldn't possibly have known this little boy or his family. Television news does this. Viewers come out to show they care. So eight hundred people sit in silence waiting for someone to stand up and start talking.

I stare straight ahead at the small dark wood coffin. There is a picture of the boy on top of the casket, which is closed. Also, a blanket of flowers falls over toward the pews. It is very formal and quiet. People cough, whisper. I sit upright on the hard wooden bench. This is real.

There is something final about this morning service that the memorial service we had for Angela Dobkin only a month ago didn't have. Angela standing outside Santa Barbara Junior High after school. Next, Angela lying on the ground, shot by her very best girlfriend.

Seventh grade can be murder.

But Angela's death was too much like what you see on television all the time. What happened to this kid came out of nowhere, was so horrible no one in his right mind could even dream it up.

I blink and look around. At least ten of us sit there in different parts of the church knowing that there is nothing, absolutely no one in that coffin.

With a direct squint that I'd been noticing for maybe a year or so, the kind that somehow expects me to understand something unsaid that will force me to ask a question or two, my dad told me autopsies take time.

Foul play. Really foul.

chapter two

There was no way any of us—Felix, Jenny, Teddy, or me—could have known what was coming.

One week, five school days before the Monday when our spring break was set to begin, half-asleep we arrived in Mr. Walston's world history class. There were two lists written on the blackboard. Here's one.

> Goodwill
> Red Cross
> Cottage Hospital
> Food Bank of Santa Barbara
> Meals on Wheels
> Senior Citizen Information Services
> Sidewalk's End
> Salvation Army
> Santa Barbara Legal Aid
> Dougherty Hospice

"Good morning, class," said Mr. Walston. A few sunbeams

fought early April mist outside our windows. Mr. Walston's horn-rimmed glasses reflected them. "Who can tell me what all these organizations have in common?"

At 7:45 on a Monday morning, no one wants to be a star.

"Come on," Walston urged, his fat hand sweeping up and down the lists. "Think."

"They're all volunteer places that help people," muttered Teddy Hines.

"Right!" Mr. Walston glowed. "Now, who can guess why I've written them on the board?"

I looked over at Teddy Hines. He's an odd kid. Not bad-looking: blond straight hair and green eyes that seem to find secret things funny. The girls whisper about him. Not just because they find him cute, I guess, but because he wears the same clothes every day.

No one seemed to care why two lists stared down at us. This didn't stop Walston. "I've made arrangements," he announced with a very proud grin, "with Macropower Computers in Goleta. They've agreed to insure you all—to underwrite you—for this project."

Project?

Each of us was to pick a spot where we would volunteer for one week. The organizations were prepared to accept our temporary help. Macropower was going to pay for anything we broke or damaged accidentally. At the end of the week, we would all have one month to write about our experiences. This paper would be worth one-half of our final grade for the year.

"We haven't yet learned too much about our country in the present, as it is now all around us," Mr. Walston explained, ignoring the seething, stone-faced statues that sat facing him, hearing our vacation explode.

I turned around to look at Felix. His eyebrows were raised

but his eyes were closed. I grinned. That was his don't-sweat-it-I'm-on-the-case expression.

"Today's problems aren't part of our studies until next year. But we're not blind. We know what's going on in California, in Santa Barbara. And it's never too early to begin trying to solve or change some of the unfairness we see all around us."

A sudden winter rainstorm was sweeping down the coast from San Francisco, chilling out all of Santa Barbara.

chapter three

"It's plain rotten," Felix sulked. "Our whole vacation ruined, shot to hell. I mean, it really torques my jaws!"

"Don't let it," Teddy Hines advised quietly. At the end of that day he was walking a step or two behind us as we pedalled shakily along at one mile an hour. "That's just the way life is."

"Well, maybe it is," Felix argued, "but I don't have to like it." Felix swung his leg off his bike. "That first week in April is ours!"

I've known Felix Maldanado since preschool. His mother, Irene, works for my dad, and has ever since I can remember. Felix is thin and sharp, a tough stringy guy who's always the first to take a dare.

"Don't fight it," Teddy said. "I mean, no one minds trying to do something good for other people. So it happens on our vacation. We'll survive. Just go with the flow."

Who cared that the seventh grade studied the Fall of Rome through the age of the Black Death, then the Renaissance? Or that by the end of the year we were supposed to have reached the writing of our own Constitution and Bill of Rights? Who cared about all that? Our Mr. Walston wanted us "engaged in the present."

"Let me tell you, man, someday I'm going to be so big, I'm going to be so important that if I don't like the flow, I can change it!"

"How?" I asked. "What are you going to be?"

"I don't know yet, just important. You wait." Felix is one confident honcho. "I'm going to stop old Walston in his tracks!"

"What do you mean?" Teddy asked.

"It's our vacation!" Felix nearly shouted. "Who does he think he is? He can't just decide to take it away from us. What about our folks, how they feel? It will seem as unfair to them as it does to us. We'll start a movement."

"It may be a little late for that," Teddy smiled.

Felix shook his head violently. "Power of the people," he explained quickly. "You wait. We start with our folks and then organize. Telephone calls, letters, threats. I'll bet you five bucks I can stop this."

"Maybe," I allowed. Felix had a lot of guts and was never afraid to shoot off his mouth. Maybe he could get us out of this. Still, just in case—"Still, Felix, just in case, what did you pick?"

"I didn't pick anything, man. I just laid back and let all you guys choose. And what was left I figured, hey, who cares? One place is as good as another. I mean, how much can one kid do in a week? What does Walston expect?" He paused and grinned. "*If* we have to do this at all."

"So what did you get?" Teddy persisted.

"Catholic Charities," Felix announced. "Everybody was afraid of that one. I'm Catholic, so what's to worry?" Felix didn't give us a lot of time to think that over. "So, Benny, what about you?" Felix was the only person in my whole life who ever called me 'Benny.'

I shrugged. "Sidewalk's End."

"The kids?" Felix sneered. "Hey, who can stand little kids screaming and fighting all day? Give me a needy Catholic any time!"

"I'd rather face little kids than old people," I said, dodging my real reason: kids are kids—homeless grown-ups scare me to death. They make me wince. I just don't want to see them. They're like land mines. Get too close, accidentally touch one, and all hell can break loose.

"Old people know everything," I added. "They make too many demands. And they don't get it."

"Get what?" asked Teddy.

"Get the difference," I explained. "The way they grew up and the way we have to. I mean, nothing is the same. They don't get it. They refuse to."

"So who made you an expert on old people?"

"I've got a grandmother, Felix. I know." I looked over at Teddy Hines. "Who'd you pick?"

Teddy hunched his shoulders so that it seemed he had no neck. "The hospice."

"The hospice?" Felix echoed. "With all those people dying? Boy, are you weird!"

Teddy smiled a little to himself. Felix saw this. "Weird, man, weird."

Teddy stopped walking. We were at the corner of Santa Barbara Street. "No, it's not," he defended softly.

"Oh no?" challenged Felix.

"No," Teddy repeated. "Look, Felix, I know about life. What I don't know about is death. Sometimes I think it may be the only really interesting thing left to learn about."

Felix stood with his jaws apart, silent.

"See you," Teddy said suddenly, peeling off and heading toward the freeway and the beach.

Felix and I watched him walk away. Then, as if we had agreed to do the same thing at the same time, we remounted our bikes and turned north.

"That guy is a banana," Felix said, starting to pump up the slight hill. "I don't know why you let him hang around."

I stood on a pedal and glided a moment. "Who knows? Maybe he's right."

"You really believe that?"

"No," I admitted.

Felix pumped, head down. His muttering drifted back to me: "Two bananas!"

chapter four

The telephone rang after dinner. My Aunt Eileen was rinsing dishes and putting them in the dishwasher. "Get it, will you, Ben, please?" she called out.

I unfolded myself from a neat cave made of pillows, Nigel our cat, and Baines our sheltie, all of us watching a Lakers game, and stood up to walk into our front hall.

It was Felix, furious. "That sneaky son-of-a-bitch!" he shouted after I said hello. I knew who he meant but I had to pretend I didn't. "Who?" I asked innocently.

"Walston! Old fat flying Walston!"

I had already discovered what Felix was going to tell me. "You know what he did?" Felix demanded.

I smiled a little. "What?"

"He went behind our backs! He got to our folks last week! And they agreed with him!"

"They did?"

"My mom says it sounds like a great idea, helping out. It will teach us understanding and sympathy! Can you believe that? He must really have done a job on them. The rain, the slides, the riots in L.A., the earthquakes. Even Angela Dobkin!"

I didn't say anything.

Felix is no fool. "Hey, Benny, you're not saying anything. You knew, didn't you? When? When?"

"Only when you did," I replied, which was true. I had told Eileen when she came back from work what was planned. She gave me the same line Felix's mom had.

"It's a plot!" Felix shouted.

"They want to keep us off the streets."

"What I don't get is why Mom didn't say anything. Or why your aunt didn't. Why the secrecy? What's going on here?"

"I think Mr. Walston asked people to hold back. Until he got everyone else's permission."

"Sure, sure! Mom said the same thing. It had to be a project for the whole class." Felix paused. "Boy, Benny, you really bought the whole line, didn't you?"

"Hey, Felix, what can we do? And how bad could it be? Besides, if it keeps raining, what else have we got to do that's better?"

"Anything! Something! It's our freedom you're talking about!"

I smiled. "Hey, it's only a week. Maybe it will be fun."

Felix choked. "Fun? I've signed up to spend five days hanging out with a bunch of wackos and you get to spend five days wiping snot from little kids. Boy, Benny, your idea of fun is really weird!"

Actually it wasn't. Felix wouldn't remember because it was all something that had happened so long ago. But I hadn't always been an only child.

Today, in our Practical Living Skills class, we study what is called a "family dynamic."

In our family, the dynamic's basic unit is One.

Now I'm an only child. My father is a single parent. My mother is a single ex-parent. I have only one grandmother left, my dad's mother. I have one aunt, Eileen, who also is single—her husband ran off even before I was born. We have one dog named Baines, and one orange mackerel cat with a ringed tail and four fluffy white feet beneath an ivory fuzzy belly, named Nigel.

I am not the kid who was supposed to "hold the marriage together." *His* name was Charley.

Philip Charles Derby.

He was the most beautiful little baby you ever saw. I have pictures of him, of both of us. We were not quite two years apart. Charley had an enormous forehead, so big all you thought of—once you got past his amazing gray eyes—was how big a brain he must have, how smart he was going to be.

What I remember best was his laugh. Charley was easy to entertain. Everything was funny to him. Nothing ever frightened him. He only cried when something really serious went wrong, like running across his playroom and falling into the corner of a table, cutting himself and bleeding all over the floor. Well, I would have cried, too.

Charley had what people call a rolling laugh. The best way I can explain it is, think of a waterfall, a fairly small one. Now think of the noise it makes. *Now* imagine that same rushing, bubbling sound, only make it musical, and make it higher by a dozen notes or so.

Then imagine no sound at all, silence.

That's what we were left with.

To this day I'm not sure exactly what happened. Sometimes I think about asking my dad but I always stop short.

I remember what I was told about it, the sort of thing you would tell any little four- or five-year-old kid about heaven and angels and God.

What I personally remember is coming back from preschool and not hearing Charley. And then being sent over to Felix's house to stay with Irene and Felix and his brother and sisters. And then, maybe three days later, coming home and still not finding Charley. Or my mother.

Maybe it's too heavy to say there are these two holes in my life, because I like the way my life is going. But sometimes, not often but just every once in a while, I find myself standing dead still, maybe in the middle of a room or even on the sidewalk outdoors. Like my grandmother going blank in the middle of a story or forgetting what she stood up to get.

I can't put my finger on something actually missing, but deep down inside, I know what it is and why I don't need to hear it labelled.

chapter five

The day after Mr. Walston's bombshell, we all had to fan out across town to visit the places where we had agreed to work.

I got to Sidewalk's End about 5:45, maybe six. I had called during lunch and made an appointment with the director.

So all innocent I arrived outside this sort of plain single-story building across the railroad tracks to find a note Scotch-taped to the front door. "Benjamin, I'm picking up a few things we need. Back in 5. Louise Denton."

The door was unlocked. I pulled it open and stepped into my own past, seeing things in the fading afternoon light that made me smile.

Alphabet letters, capitals and lowercase, were taped along the walls. Smeared finger-paintings hung in clumps on wallboard. Stacks of boxes lined up neatly or placed one on top of the other were filled with clothing and toys.

From where I stood, just at the entrance of a big space for playing, I could also practice my basic Spanish. A lot of diagrams and signs were in two languages. I was getting my tongue around a phrase on a poster when I *heard* something from my past, too: the sound of a scurrying, snuffling, restless animal. The school pet, cute and snuggly.

The noise made me grin. I remembered guinea pigs and gerbils spinning on their own tails, clean, soft little animals purposely designed for kids.

I walked slowly toward the scratching noise and saw a cage maybe two feet long, one foot high, one foot wide. It was filled with torn newspaper and faded, wilting lettuce leaves. I bent down in the half-darkness to get a closer look.

I stood up so quickly you'd have thought I'd been shot!

Somebody had to be kidding!

An ordinary brown, shiny, slick and sharp-toothed California sewer rat was in that cage!

Gross!

It sat on its hind legs, silent and still, staring back up at me. Its whiskers quivered.

Somebody's crazy around here! *This* is no pet for little kids, kids who probably wake screaming in the middle of the night as one of its big ugly cousins scrambles across their covers. Or worse, their legs.

Rats had carried the bubonic plague across Europe in the Middle Ages. Rats and their fleas and germs caused the deaths of millions of people, children and grown-ups.

Who's the bozo here?

What had happened to the world's supply of pink-eyed, fuzzy, cuddly white rabbits? Or gerbils and guinea pigs, white mice or even chipmunks and squirrels?

I heard someone behind me. I blinked, straightened, and spun around, in no mood for another gigantic surprise.

Gigantic?

There she stood, all six feet, one hundred and ten pounds of her!

She wore something that looked like a multicolored curtain, loose and long. If she'd raised her arms I would have screamed.

Didn't this woman eat? She was so thin and so tall that after a second all I could think of was a piece of stiff uncooked pasta on wheels.

I looked up at her. What else could I do?

She smiled.

Amazing! Her smile was so welcoming and hopeful that she seemed to shrink almost to normal size. Still smiling, she motioned me to take one of the baby chairs that was set against a baby table. She did the same.

"I'm sorry I wasn't here to greet you," she said, her voice light and open, used to delivering happy news, "but I'm glad you read my note and came in, anyway." She paused for a moment. I wasn't sure whether to speak. "Now, Benjamin, why did you choose us?"

I didn't know how truthful to be. I didn't say anything. I just tried to smile as happily as she had, hoping that would be answer enough.

"Benjamin, there must have been a reason. What was it that made you volunteer for Sidewalk's End?"

"Children," I whispered.

Ms. Louise Denton smiled broadly–she hadn't stopped smiling! "That's why I'm here, too. Good. It's nice to know someone your age is so mature."

I know flattery when I hear it. I like it.

"We open every day at seven-thirty," Ms. Denton began to explain. "We're here until five-thirty. Parents bring their children and sign them in. It's a rule. And they must sign them out. Everything we do here at Sidewalk's End is for the children. Everything."

I nodded.

"We never discipline a child, Benjamin. We persuade. We

try to explain, to redirect their thoughts or actions. Sometimes that's not easy."

Behind Ms. Denton, leaning up against a shelf of pillows and picture books, was a plastic machine gun. "What about that?" I asked, pointing.

She turned. "Well, today that's part of everyone's world, I'm sorry to say. We get donations. All kinds of toys and food and clothing. But if a child picked that up and aimed it threateningly at another child, I would say something like, 'Oh Benjamin, we don't need to do that. We don't need to play that way. Why don't we go over here and draw some pictures?' We deflect, if you understand."

"You wouldn't say that it was dangerous to point a gun? Or that a gun isn't something we should play with?"

"I might. The trouble is, Ben, that any child who watches a lot of television knows what that gun is for and how to use it."

"I don't understand why you keep it around."

"We're not here to hide reality from children, Ben, but to help them understand it."

I thought maybe that made sense. Maybe. "Couldn't I just say no?"

"You could, but it's better to add something useful. It's something you'll learn to do."

"In one week?"

Louise Denton nodded. "Even in one week. I know you can do it. Do you have any questions you'd like to ask?"

One, anyway. Whose terrific idea was *that* thing–caged in the corner, rummaging and scavenging and scarfing up everything that wasn't chained down?

"Are the kids here healthy?"

Ms. Denton's eyes widened. "Why? Are you afraid of catching something?

I shrugged. "I just wondered."

"Some of our children are underfed, tired. Some need a bath. All need care and comfort and a chance to grow. Which is exactly what this program offers their parents, too. A few hours to look for work, to look for housing, to get counselling. We give parents time for themselves, time they can use to regroup, recharge their batteries."

"How many are crazy?"

"Benjamin! What a question." Ms. Denton *nearly* frowned. "And whom do you mean? The children or their parents?"

"Their parents."

Ms. Denton crossed her very long legs. She put up a bony finger to her nose and turned sideways in thought for a second. Her nose was long like the rest of her, with a hump in its middle. "Benjamin, have you ever been hassled by someone on the street?"

"Well, you have to admit there are some pretty scary-looking people out there. I mean, well, no, nothing's ever happened to me but–but it could! Like everybody else, Ms. Denton, I try to keep my distance."

"'Lou', Benjamin. Please. Call me 'Lou'. But if you haven't had a bad experience, why should you expect one now?"

"I don't expect it," I answered. "But I don't want to be surprised, either. I mean, those gonzos are likely to go off at any minute."

Lou Denton nodded. "That's one of our biggest problems. What people think they see. But, Ben, the number of homeless people who *are* crazy, or too alone or off-balance more than the rest of us, is very small. Truly."

"Maybe, but sometimes it seems there are more of them than us."

"Ben, this isn't an us-and-them kind of thing. Believe me. With the wrong set of circumstances, every one of us could be out on the street."

A telephone rang somewhere in the building. Lou Denton ignored it. It rang a couple more times and then I could hear a switch cut off the signal and a recording machine go into action.

"Here's what you have to keep in mind, Ben," Ms. Denton said next. She put her hands on her knees and leaned toward me like she was sharing a secret. "It's children you volunteered to help. They're not crazy. They're just little kids easy to love and who will love you back, I know."

Ms. Denton put her weight on her hands and stood up. "And any parent you meet here is likely to be as concerned as we both are about how to make their children's lives better. There's nothing to fear, believe me."

A hand was floating in front of my chest. This was the end of our interview. "Ben, I'm glad you want to help. I know you'll have fun. Be brave, and relax."

She broke our handshake and ruffled the top of my head. "See you Monday morning. We'll talk more then."

I tried to smile confidently.

I wanted to be around little kids like Charley, help take care of them. But how could I concentrate when every day right in front of my eyes a grungy little furball, all sharp teeth and germs, scurried around inside, hungry for its chance to take a chunk out of a tiny finger or hand? When every day *outside* you saw what these kids might grow up to be?

chapter six

My dad has two attitudes about the homeless. One is fuzzy and sort of good-hearted: they're down on their luck, they need a helping hand, we should offer one. So at the end of every day he sends leftover food to one shelter or another and then feels good about himself.

On the other hand, his restaurant is right on State Street. It has a big patio behind adobe walls and an entryway that's open and inviting. Tourists and people from Santa Barbara peek in, getting sucked into the scene by music and videos and the smell of hot spiced beef and tacos. The place fills up and then, wham! When you least expect it, some skanky-looking wreck creeps in and hits someone up for a cigarette or a dollar and then magically disappears. And sometimes right after that, so do my dad's customers. It drives him wild.

When Dad rants and raves about trying to do business in a town that's full of cadging bums, my Aunt Eileen gets so worked up about the plight of the homeless and their families that she can hardly stay in the same room with him. Sometimes

I get the feeling she's right on the edge of really laying my dad out.

My dad is a basic good guy. Maybe in *his* Practical Skills classes he learned how to understand what he feels and when to say it. He's not afraid to tell me he loves me. And he's not afraid to tell me I have disappointed him, admitting sometimes that his expectations are pretty high. With praise he's quick and, I think, sincere.

He's not the most educated guy around. He went to college but he never finished. He has a big smile, a big voice, and big hands that gently help a woman into a chair or knock some male customer's shoulder good-naturedly.

Dad dates. I don't see every woman, but I know, and Eileen does, when it's happening.

He dresses well and he keeps in shape. He'll go bicycling with me when the weather's fine. In the rain, he bicycles and works out in his bedroom.

Rain is what fell all weekend before spring break. It was tough to plan what to do with my final two days of freedom–hanging out at Hendry's Beach wouldn't be any fun, and biking into the country was out. I'm not a rich kid to begin with, and since it was the weekend, most of my allowance had disappeared, keeping me out of the malls.

Felix and I just lay around, either at my house or at his, watching sports on television and every so often wandering through his kitchen or mine to see if there was something we had missed that might be worth eating.

I honestly didn't think I was worried about anything, but on Sunday night, when I closed my eyes, all I could imagine was how everything at Sidewalk's End could go wrong, no matter how hard I tried to help–kids getting lost, fire, plague, vermin.

Especially vermin. One particular rat. Who knew how big *his* family unit was?

My first day of spring break. There I am, about six-thirty in the morning, biking down a deserted State Street toward the beach. In my windbreaker's pocket is Aunt Eileen's usual list of things to get on my way home. The streets are still damp from the weekend rains, and the mist above my head looks more like rain clouds than fog.

Sidewalk's End is in a neighborhood that has both houses and hotels, factories and stores. It's about two blocks from the waterfront and an equal distance from the nearest green park with huge fig trees. I guess it makes sense to put a place offering help between the water and the railroad tracks, since that's where most homeless people hang out.

I was supposed to arrive a little early so that Lou Denton could give me some more instruction. Actually, I figured it was to grill me again.

"Hi, Ben," she said as I walked in through the front door. "I like a dependable worker."

"Hello, Ms. Denton."

"'Lou', please, Ben. I told you."

I didn't think I would ever be able to toss her name off like that. But I nodded.

"Come on in. Let's talk."

I followed her into the main playroom, thinking that she looked sort of like a stork–long and tall and loose-limbed, dressed today in darker clothes than before but still winged. It was amazing how easily she could fold herself down into one of the center's tiny chairs.

"Nervous?" she asked first.

"A little."

"Good. You should be. Taking care of children is always a responsibility. Now, I'm not going to give you any particular assignment, Ben. You'll meet our other teacher soon, and today we have a volunteer from City College scheduled to work, too. All week you'll see people coming in to help, other volunteers. I think you'll like them and I know they'll be pleased to find you here."

I nodded. I was doing a lot of nodding.

"Just by being alert and keeping your eyes open, Ben, you'll see where you're needed and what to do. The children will teach you, trust me."

It was the rat I didn't trust. I looked across the room at his cage. I wanted to suggest that maybe he should be poisoned, or burned, or tortured to death.

"Just to make you feel a little easier about all this, Ben, you won't be alone at any time. There will always be someone else around to help or to ask questions of. Oh, and I think I should tell you that we have one child, Stephanie, who probably won't pay any attention to you. Don't be disappointed or angry, Ben. She shies away from any man who works here, no matter what age."

She paused.

"Why?" I helped.

Ms. Denton smiled. I wondered whether she practiced smiling every night when she got home. How could this much happiness be real? "Well, we're not sure yet, Ben. We think she was a drug baby. I mean, her mother may have been using during her pregnancy. Worse, we think Stephanie probably has a history of being abused."

"How old is she?"

"Just two."

Something zapped me, something hazy and steamy and,

strangely, white. I was lost for a second in time. I blinked myself back. "Wow. Poor kid."

"Actually, Ben, we think she's doing remarkably. She's still willing to climb onto our laps and let us hug her. And she plays well with the other children. She's just uncomfortable around men."

"How will I recognize her?"

"You will, believe me. She's tiny, of course, and she has a pale little heart-shaped face. Her hair is brown and cut in bangs. She'll look at you, probably a hundred times, but she won't come near. I just don't want you to be personally upset by this."

"No," I said. "I won't. I get it."

"Good," Ms. Denton said, once more putting her hands on her knees to push up into a standing position.

"All right. People will be arriving soon. Just wander around and make yourself familiar with everything. And, Ben, trust your instincts. I will."

I nodded and gave a little smile. That was a nice thing to say.

It was just after seven.

I ignored the cage.

The layout was fairly simple. You walked through two doors. Ms. Denton's office was on the left; a few paces beyond was a doorway that led into a room where there were cribs set up, and a table for changing a baby's diapers. On this room's far wall was another doorway that led out into the gravelled play area, which was jammed with standing toys–things to climb on, to ride on, to hide in, to swing from. The whole yard couldn't have been more than a hundred square feet.

Back inside, there was a big kitchen with a gigantic refrigerator and a stove almost like what my dad has in his restaurant: cast-iron and heavy-duty. There was a stainless steel counter running through the middle of the room, and cupboards lined every wall surface. Two deep sinks stood side by side under a window.

Near the bathroom was a desk that had an open book on its top where parents signed in and out twice a day. All kinds of literature was spread out there, too: how to find shelter, job counseling, health matters, parenting.

Turning right, you enter into a world of remembered colors. Everything you ever saw when you were a kid is sitting there, waiting: Tinkertoys, Erector sets, wooden trains, books and crayons, balls and dolls, pickup sticks, toy trucks and vans, wooden blocks that get bigger and bigger for building something.

The playroom was a large open space where I guessed—because of a huge cushy rug in its center—meetings or classes were held. Here too was the table around which a dozen little kids could sit to have breakfast or lunch.

A huge mound of building blocks stood next to the library, where hundreds of picture books were lined up, most of them looking pretty well used.

Another section of the big room, this one up a step and without windows, was for naptime. Little area rugs were scattered about, and leaning against the walls were blankets and pillows and soft plush toys for cradling close.

The real day began as a thin black woman in jeans walked in with her child—a little girl dressed as though she were going to a tea party at Buckingham Palace, frilled and bowed and shined bright—and the other teacher arrived. She came directly at me, *her* smile wide and her hand outstretched in my direction. "Ben, right?" she guessed.

I nodded and shook her hand. She didn't look a lot older than I was. She was definitely prettier.

"I'm Debbie," she announced. "Glad you're here. We can really use you."

Before I could think what to say, she whirled around and knelt, holding out her arms to the beautiful little black doll who toddled toward her. "LaKesha!" Debbie called. She scooped up the bundle of lace and curls and threw her toward the ceiling. The little girl squealed happily.

And then, faster than I could count, the place was teeming with kids.

For a while I stood as still as the leg of a pier with water swirling below it. Child after child rushed into the playroom toward a toy or a friend. I didn't know what to do so I didn't do anything.

Some kids went right to work, taking things apart, sitting on the floor with a toy between their legs and crooning. There were a couple of early-morning tussles over favorite toys or books. I watched Debbie bending down and standing up, it seemed like a hundred different times. Ms. Denton talked to adults as they came in to sign the register. In the kitchen I spied a woman I hadn't seen arrive, cutting things up and organizing, putting equal parts of something into bowls.

I moved off to the side of the playroom, trying to stay out of the way and yet look involved, waiting for a chance to be helpful.

It came. A bright-eyed little boy came barreling into the playroom and took a real header. He wasn't hurt so much as startled, and he pulled himself up to sit on the carpet, crying. I took a few steps forward and knelt down in front of him, reaching out to tie his right shoe.

The little boy stopped crying. Not in thanks. Probably in surprise. He hadn't seen *me* before. Who was this person? I didn't say anything. I just smiled and stood, taking his hand and gently pulling him up. Within a couple more seconds, he was off, doing whatever he wanted, this new person forgotten or at least put into the back of his mind for later.

Then I saw her.

Stephanie.

She was crouched across the room, her hand on the binding of a big picture book. She looked surprised. She was staring at me.

Her face *was* heart-shaped. And her forehead was topped by bangs, thin brown hair flopping toward her eyes.

What surprised me was how old she looked. Ms. Denton had said she was two. To me she looked more like fifty. She was horribly thin, although she was dressed warmly. Her wrists couldn't have been more than two inches around, and her face had hollows at her cheeks and under her eyes. She looked like what people mean when they say "anemic," too pale and with skin so thin you think you can see through it to the bone.

She didn't blink, her hand motionless in midair against the shelf of books. She didn't turn away after a second, the way you might have expected her to. Her pale blue eyes were steady, almost as though she were on some inner alert.

Remembering what Ms. Denton had told me, I smiled carefully back at her and then turned away, hearing two high-voiced little Hispanic kids in midwrestle.

I knelt down and tried to separate them gently, saying something—I can't remember what—in English or in Spanish, trying to send them into neutral corners to neutral toys. I succeeded. They didn't know who I was but they knew I was stronger than they were. They stopped grappling and looked at me, and then at each other. Finally, best friends in the world, they tottered off toward the wire cage atop the table in the corner. I stood up, feeling proud of myself.

Oh no! One of the two was just tall enough to get his fingers through the mesh of the cage's door.

"Esteban!"

Debbie had seen him, too. "We'll take Buster out after lunch, O.K.?"

Esteban pulled his tiny hand back from the cage and down a bit, looking disappointed.

I was not.

Then I felt it.

It was "them."

Stephanie's two arms.

Wrapped around my knees.

chapter seven

I looked down, startled. She was holding on to me and, with her head against my leg, smiling up into my face.

No kidding.

I didn't want to frighten her. I didn't want to make any sudden moves, like swooping down to try to pick her up. But I have to admit I was kind of pleased.

Maybe I shouldn't have been. Stephanie at my knees was telling me she wasn't afraid of me–didn't *need* to be afraid. I wasn't big enough or old enough or strong enough or scary-enough-looking.

I wasn't really a man yet.

That idea didn't thrill me, but I had it, just the same.

I smiled back down at her for a second, and then, ever so gently, so she wouldn't think I didn't like her, I began to pull out of her reach.

Stephanie sat back on her heels and watched, still keeping her eyes on mine, and smiling, just a little. It seemed to me she was signalling that she understood exactly what I was doing and why, and that it was O.K. with her. Maybe she had been running a test. I passed, I think.

The third woman–whose name turned out to be Freida and who was as old as Ms. Denton and Debbie put together–came out of the kitchen then. "Who wants breakfast?" she asked in English. Another voice–Debbie's or Ms. Denton's–echoed the question in Spanish.

The whole flock ran to line up outside the bathroom to wash hands, then dashed back to wait eagerly for Freida as she started bringing cereal bowls to the table.

Breakfast consisted of cold cereal with milk, white toast and butter, orange juice, and tiny pieces of fruit, all cut up and divided to fit tiny fingers.

I was beginning to feel more comfortable. I sat between two-year-olds, alternately helping to spoon in and wipe up, side to side. I also began to memorize names.

Stephanie was burned into my mind. LaKesha was still picture-book perfect. Esteban and his best pal, Miguel, were both just under three and happy as I've ever seen little kids be. Miguel had long dark hair and baggy jeans; Esteban had short dark hair and overalls.

There was a tough-looking little boy named Wendell. His long fair hair fell toward his eyes which were bright blue but also flashed a warning all the time. I got the impression he was one spoiled kid just looking for someone to cross him. He was three and he could talk, clearly. I was also sure he could punch if he had to.

Next to him sat a girl of four, dressed neatly without too many frills. I remembered that she had arrived holding on to her grandmother's hand. She had long brown hair tied in a ponytail and seemed very tall for her age. I didn't like her.

I don't know why. Even now I can't imagine what I had

against her, or Wendell. But I didn't feel guilty. I mean, there are people you like right away and there are those you don't. Barbara was one I didn't.

Breakfast ended. Freida came back with a big plastic bag to collect the paper plates and used napkins and spoons. The kids stood up and moved as a group onto the center rug, sprawling there, waiting.

"Would you like to read, Benjamin?" Ms. Denton asked.

I shook my head. While I didn't feel like an outsider anymore, I also wasn't confident enough to want to stand in any part of a spotlight.

So Ms. Denton selected a picture book and sat cross-legged on the floor. I sat to her left, my legs straight out and crossed at the ankles. Debbie was next to me. Before Ms. Denton even opened the book, Miguel and Esteban had situated themselves on my legs, sitting on them as though they were on top of horses. This naturally brought horses to *my* mind, so I began to bounce them slowly, flexing and bending my knees a little to a rhythm that was gentle but occasionally surprising. Both boys giggled softly as Ms. Denton began to read.

I have no idea what the story was that morning. I was somewhere else. Actually, I think I was with Miguel and Esteban, being bounced–Charley and me–on Dad's legs. Ms. Denton's voice was calm and low-pitched, rising whenever the story was supposed to be exciting or funny. All of us kids just sat there around her, listening or daydreaming, looking up whenever she turned the pages of the book around to show us a picture.

After storytime we were told to put on our jackets and sweaters for a walk. Ms. Denton packed a paper bag with snacks and paper napkins, and told me to carry two big rubber balls.

There were twelve kids (some I haven't mentioned) and three adults. I counted myself in the grown-up category, no matter what Stephanie thought.

Before we could set out, though, through the front door in a baby carriage came a thirteenth client: huge brown eyes, the longest eyelashes I had ever seen outside a zoo (the llama is what I mean), a bright red dress over diapers and leggings, and more toys hanging from the frame of her carriage than you ever saw dangling above the dashboard of any low-rider. Dolores, not yet two years old.

She didn't get there alone, of course. Her grandmother was wheeling her—a tiny, bronze, wrinkled woman with sharp flat eyes like a bird's.

Just what we needed. With three of us around, we had some chance of controlling and keeping up with twelve toddlers. But with one person assigned to push Dolores in her carriage, that meant twelve little demons on the rampage chased by only two grown-ups. Suddenly I wasn't so anxious for fresh air.

chapter eight

Within about thirty seconds after leaving Sidewalk's End, we were strung out along the sidewalk like cars in a train. Ms. Denton—"Lou"—had three kids by the hand—which is to say she held the hands of two little kids and a third was attached to one of these. I was behind her with my own gaggle of kids, four, two of whom carried a ball. Fenced in by our two groups were five temporarily well-behaved three-year-olds. Bringing up the rear was Debbie, pushing Dolores in her baby-carriage.

We trooped along Yanapali Street toward Pershing Park in a fairly orderly way. When we reached corners, cars automatically stopped for us, waiting patiently for Debbie to push the carriage up the sloping curve of a handicapped ramp. No horns; no shouts. It all reminded me of a book that had been read over and over to me when I was little, a book with pictures of a whole string of baby ducks trailing their mother through a park in Boston.

Everything was orderly until we crossed the last street before the greenery of the park, and then the kids flew in all directions.

Four ran directly to an enormous tree that overlooked one of the baseball fields that belonged to Santa Barbara College. They were too small to climb it, but big enough to scramble around its gnarled trunk. This would have been fine, but there was broken glass and empty beer cans and a lot of other junk I won't even describe strewn around the tree's base. A lot of this was dangerous, of course, so I was bending and grabbing, reaching and lifting, pocketing and hiding at the same time that I was pretending to be having as much fun as the kids.

Actually, I was. While I hoisted and pushed and lifted, a black four-year-old named Max shimmied up to a branch to call out military-style commands in his hoarse, surprisingly deep voice. Max was dressed in cowboy boots. Maybe he thought they gave him extra authority. Most of his troop ignored him.

Debbie settled under another tree with Dolores in her carriage. She had brought a picture book with her and had tiny listeners nearby. Ms. Denton walked to the steps of a bandshell, where she spread out her snacks and where Wendell was tanking up.

I ambled around, trying to keep within reach or at least within shouting distance of the kids near me. From the corner of my eye I saw Stephanie running across the grass at one side of the bandshell, headed who knew where but all on her own. I chased her and, when she saw me about to reach out to catch her, she stopped and fell to the ground, grinning up at me and rolling over on her back. I lifted her up, put her on her feet, and pointed her in Ms. Denton's direction.

I heard a tiny shout and turned to see Batista, a round, muscular little kid, kick one of the rubber balls over the fence onto the baseball field. Swell. I walked over and slipped through the fence to retrieve it. I tossed it back to Batista who,

to my complete amazement, headed it as though he were playing soccer and then chased it, kicking it the same way. The kid
had talent.

I walked nearer to watch him. He had a contented smile on
his face and he was breathing hard as he chased the ball. He was
round and fully packed because of the diapers beneath his
jeans. The bottoms of his pants were rolled up, and their waist
clung to his tiny hips, threatening to collapse around his ankles
at every step. He had wonderful curly hair and eyes that looked
a little like what I thought an Eskimo's eyes would look
like–brown and thin-lidded and slanted. They weren't slanted,
they just looked that way.

Wendell shot by me then, chasing the second ball, with
Esteban hot on his trail. I strolled along after them, keeping an
eye on Batista and Stephanie as best I could.

"You must be Ben."

I looked over my shoulder to see a guy not much taller
than I was but a whole lot thinner. He had brown hair tied back
behind his ears and an earring in his left lobe. He wore cut-offs
and a sweatshirt that was so faded I couldn't read what had
once been printed on it. He wore hornrimmed glasses and a
baseball cap reversed.

"My name is Frank," he said, sticking out his hand. "Francisco really, but 'Frank' is easier to remember."

I shook his hand.

"Glad you could spend some time with us. We need all the
help we can get."

Oh. "Are you a volunteer?" I asked.

He nodded. "I'm at the College, studying family counselling," he replied, walking along by my side as we watched
the kids ahead of us.

"How long have you been working here?"

"About six months. I come down whenever I have time, not just for the kids but to talk with their parents, too. It's helpful in my courses."

This was interesting. "Do you know about their families? I mean, do you know, for example, about Wendell or LaKesha's folks?"

"Some. Wendell's a tough little guy on top but very nervous underneath. He lives with his family in a welfare hotel. Not a place you'd choose for a kid, let me tell you. As a matter of fact, at naptime we wake Wendell first. It was his mother's idea. The hotel's so noisy that if Wendell really got a good rest at Sidewalk's End, he'd never be able to sleep at night."

"What about Max's family?"

"It depends. When Max's dad is around, we never see Max. When he's gone, Max shows up like clockwork."

"Why?"

"Max's mother. She's afraid of her husband so she does whatever he tells her. When he gets out of jail, he wants Max with him all the time. Even though his mother knows he's better off here with us, she gives in. Then when the old man gets hauled in again, her common sense returns and so does Max."

"Why does he go to jail?"

Frank shrugged. "Little things. But always just big enough or serious enough to get him arrested."

Batista's ball flew by then and Frank reached out quickly with his foot and caught it, dribbled it a second and then fired it back. Batista caught it like a pro, turning and dribbling across the grass.

"And Stephanie?" I asked.

"She's coming along," Frank told me. "It's a tough call. We have to report abuse when we see it. It's our duty. But sometimes it's invisible. Other times you can tell clearly—bruises and cuts and whatnot."

We both heard a whistle and turned. Ms. Denton was signalling.

We walked back together toward the bandshell and collected all the soft-drink cartons and fruit peels and napkins and threw them into a trash can.

"I think it's warm enough to go to the beach, don't you, Frank?" she asked.

A dozen kids on the loose in a small park was one thing, but on a huge beach at the edge of the ocean?

Was I the only adult around who thought of these things?

Even though we had to make our way across Cabrillo Boulevard, which is a highway, we made it safely. About twenty yards onto the sand was a play area, with a steel construction that had a slide, a barrel for hiding, stairs for climbing, and bars for swinging from. The kids were in heaven. Or would have been if most of them could have reached anything. They couldn't. I could. Frank could. Debbie and Ms. Denton could. So for an hour we lifted and shifted and pushed by the seat of the pants; we carried and caught and encouraged to be brave. We wiped tears and noses and tucked in shirts and took off shoes. The sun broke through and so did sweat.

It was nearly one o'clock when we started back to Sidewalk's End. I had Wendell by the hand. He was not happy. He must have figured out that I wasn't his greatest fan because, as our troop wandered along the sidewalk, he dragged and dawdled. There was a cement barrier between the sidewalk and the beach and he had to walk along its top. O.K. by me. But he kept jumping over its side onto the sand, playing there on his hands and knees.

About five minutes after setting out, we were a hundred feet behind the group. Ten minutes and we were two hundred behind. I was losing my patience.

"Come on, Wendell. Let's catch up. I'll race you."

I climbed onto the cement barricade myself and started out a step ahead of him. I ran maybe five or six paces and stopped to look behind me. Wendell had jumped off again and, ignoring me, was happily puttering around in the sand. Terrific.

I leapt over onto the sand again to grab him. "Now, Wendell, come on. We'll miss lunch."

No response. No extra speed, either.

I reached for his hand and started to lead him, picking up my pace just a bit. He slipped out of my grip and jumped back onto the beach.

I vaulted after and nailed him. I lifted him over the runner and deposited him on the sidewalk, holding his hand very firmly. Darkly he looked up at me and put his feet out ahead of his body, skidding along as I tried to get him to walk to catch up with everyone else.

"Look, dude," I said angrily, "I am not kidding!"

A strange look flashed across his face and suddenly he walked!

I didn't say anything more. I was afraid to. I had accidently found a key. Someone he knew, when angry, called him "dude," and he was frightened. I felt I had accidentally opened the wrong door and looked into a room filled with shadows and objects I hadn't ever wanted to see.

Lunch was melted cheese sandwiches and ice cream. I had a thought about the kind of stuff Sidewalk's End served to the kids, but I decided to keep it to myself.

Naptime!

The kids knew what to do. Each ran to get his or her tiny mattress or pad, and blanket and pillow. Then they slipped off their shoes, knotting laces more than untying, and placed them neatly at the end of their mats.

Next it was a run to the bookshelves, a run back, and waving hands for someone to read them to sleep.

Esteban nailed me.

I stretched out beside him and pulled his blanket over his legs. He held a counting book up to me and I took it. I leaned on an elbow and opened its pages.

"'One is the number we think of when we think about ourselves,'" the text began.

Wait a minute! I said to myself. That's not nice. That's downright selfish. Numero Uno and screw you! What are we teaching here?

I made up my own text.

But within a few seconds I understood that Esteban didn't care at all what I was pretending to read. He also didn't understand it. Oh. O.K.

"*Uno*," I said, pointing to the large red figure.

He smiled sweetly.

I turned the page. "¿*Dos*?"

I think he nodded but I'm not sure. What he did do was nestle into his pillow and close his eyes, lying on his back with his hands folded very properly on his chest. I got to "*tres*," and then on as far as "*ocho*" before I knew he was off to dreamland.

I looked around the nap area. Debbie was with Wendell, reading to him in a whisper and stroking his arm at the same time. Frank was at LaKesha's side, leaning on his elbow, too. Ms. Denton sat between Max and Barbara, reading. They were leaning up on their elbows, hands to ears, to see the pages. There was classical music playing softly on a radio, and the kids who weren't being read to paged through books on their own, understanding as much or as little as they were used to doing. Some happy children, exhausted from all the outdoor activity, sank immediately into dreaming, on their stomachs or sides, mouths open, completely still but for their breathing. It was the best time of day.

I stood up carefully so as not to jostle Esteban. I tiptoed into the kitchen. Ms. Denton followed. "Well, Ben, how's it going? Having fun?"

"It's hard work!"

"But doesn't it make you feel good? You've been a tremendous help all day. I'm glad you chose us."

Flattery again. I liked it even more.

By the end of the week, it would be hard to remember how easily I had been pleased.

chapter nine

The afternoon ended quickly. The kids got up from their naps a little after three to be given another snack of fruit and cookies and milk. Then Esteban and Miguel, remembering what Debbie had said so many hours earlier, ran toward the cage.

The other kids followed. I didn't. I watched from a healthy distance of about twenty feet.

Debbie crossed the big space to join them and opened the cage. "Barbara, it's your turn, I think," she said. Barbara reached bravely into the cage with both hands and lifted the rat out. She put him down gently on the table and left one hand near him, fingers flat to the wood, so he could crawl around over them. Her eyes followed the little scavenger almost lovingly. I broke into a sweat.

Then Miguel put his arm on the table and the rat sniffed him before running halfway up and then swiftly back down again. Miguel giggled at the touch.

Other hands reached out to be sniffed, or to pet. Every so often I heard an "ohhh!" or a squeal. The kids were fascinated by this beast. They seemed to think he was a normal pet, furry and cuddly and cute. All I could think of was germs.

"O.K.," Debbie said after a few moments, "let's put Buster back in his cage now."

Barbara did the honors. She picked him up carefully and eased him slowly through the wire door. When the door was secured again, half a dozen sets of fingers waved through the mesh until Debbie said, "All right, let Buster catch his breath."

So the group turned almost as one and ran out into the side play-yard, where Max took charge of organizing the activity from the seat of a tiny bicycle that was stabilized by rusted training wheels.

Once again I was lifting and carrying, or pushing and catching. Happily for me, the first parent arrived exactly at five-thirty. LaKesha's father, a huge black man with a beard, came into the hallway to sign her out.

Other parents showed up; the most interesting—to me—was a beautiful woman, dressed very neatly in a pretty blouse and creased slacks, her hair neat and pulled back, her face clear and showing just the tiniest traces of makeup.

"Who's that?" I asked Frank.

"Miguel's mother," he told me.

"But she doesn't look…you know…"

Frank nodded. "Homeless? You know, Ben, there are parents who bring their kids here who have real jobs and real responsibilities. What they haven't got just at this precise moment is enough money for a place to live."

"But if they have jobs and are being paid…?"

Frank smiled. "It's not something someone your age would think about, Ben. But to get an apartment, more often than not you need to make a deposit. You need to put up one month's rent in advance, and often the last month's rent, too. Sometimes that can add up to a thousand dollars or more."

"So, does Miguel's mother have a job?"

Frank nodded. "She works in a doctor's office."

"Where does she live?"

"In a shelter. She'll stay as long as she can and try to save enough money so that when her stay is over, she can rent someplace."

"Who tells her when her stay's over?"

Frank shrugged. "Sometimes the shelter, sometimes social services. It isn't easy being homeless, Ben, let me tell you," he added with a crazy sort of smile. "I mean, there are *rules*."

"See you tomorrow, Ben!" Ms. Denton called out to me as I threw my leg over the seat of my bicycle. I waved and pushed off, pedalling north on State Street, through the underpass, wondering what Felix's day at Catholic Charities had been like, whether he felt as good, as useful as I did.

Suddenly I remembered the list of things Aunt Eileen had given me the night before. I pulled the folded paper out of my jacket pocket and looked at it. Nothing too heavy. Good.

I took a left and rode a block over to Chapala to a bodega there. It was a small store, run by a Chicano family, but it usually had whatever Aunt Eileen needed. Actually it wasn't much different from a regular supermarket except in size. It had aisles and carts and stacks of stuff in every corner.

I was nosing around slowly, in the back part of the store, trying to find the kind of spaghetti sauce Eileen wanted–she's very particular about which kind she likes to doctor up–when I heard a cry that made me shiver. I wheeled around and looked up the aisle towards the front of the store.

Batista was flying through the air backward!

I ran forward as fast as I could. He had flown from my left to my right, and I had heard him land on top of something with a loud crash and a huge scream.

By the time I rounded the corner of the aisle, Batista was standing up sobbing, tears streaming down his cheeks, cans of Italian tomatoes scattered all around him. Just then I was pushed out of the way by a woman I'd never seen before, who I guessed was Batista's mother. She knelt down in front of him, her hands on both his shoulders, and said something in a whisper to him. I couldn't hear it but he sure did. He froze.

A cart edged my leg, pushed by another child. She looked a little like Batista so I figured this was his sister. Before I had much time to think about what was going on, though, Batista's mother stood up and grabbed his hand. In Spanish much too fast for me to understand she said something to a man behind the cash register and hauled Batista out toward the sidewalk.

I was cemented to the floor. Finally I put my spaghetti sauce on a pile of canned peaches and slipped out of the store.

I hadn't been able to hear what the woman had whispered to Batista, but it had sure scared the hell out of him. Whatever it was had been short and threatening, a warning. Like what we've all heard someone else's mother–maybe even our own–say in anger: "You want something to *really* cry about?"

In my heart of hearts I was convinced Batista was going to get more of where that had come from, and I wanted to see it. I wanted to stop it. I had to!

chapter ten

I stood on the sidewalk near my bike and all I could think of was Hit-and-Run.

Because Batista and his mother and his sister had disappeared. They must have had a get-away car idling at the curb.

I guess I wasn't thinking clearly. I got on my bike and drove all the way around the block twice, looking for them. At last I started up Chapala Street, pedalling almost blindly and not stopping for lights or even flashing red signs. I was lucky traffic was thin and drivers were defensive, because I was chugging away in a fog.

I tried to reason with myself. Maybe I was being too dramatic. Maybe Batista wasn't so much afraid of his mother as he was startled by what had happened to him. I mean, little kids sometimes cry for their own reasons, not grown-up ones.

But all I could think of was his flying figure in midair and then crashing, screaming.

In the back of my mind something I couldn't control was trying to surface. It wasn't anything that had happened to me personally. It was more like something from the past I had heard about. Ideas clashed in my mind, as though they were bits and pieces of a ship, say, smashed on the rocks, little signs of human life floating to the top of the water, swirling there, waiting to be read, or assembled, like clues to a mystery.

Something else nudged, too, something I had read or heard or been told. I couldn't clear the static in my brain until I was almost home, and then the message came through loud and clear. It was what Frank had told me while we were in the park. About duty. His duty. And now, clearly, mine.

I leaned my bicycle against the side of the house and went around to the front door. Just inside, waiting and eager, was Baines, shedding long sheltie wool, dancing up to me and then dancing away toward an umbrella stand in which was his leash. He goes through this routine every day, rain or shine. He never seems to understand that before I can take him out for watering, I have to get down on my hands and knees and greet Nigel.

Nigel is a people-cat. Not that he's so terrifically smart. He doesn't, after all, speak. But he is happiest when someone is around to pay attention to him. If he feels ignored, he takes action. The big wing chair in the corner of our living room is where he takes revenge. He walks right over to it, looks back at the offending personality, and then claws whatever he can reach.

In order to keep Nigel happy, I developed a greeting ceremony: I get down on my hands and knees and he comes up to me and we rub heads. I speak in a tiny squeaky voice and he squeaks back in his tiny voice. When he's had enough, he gives me his backside and walks away contentedly toward the kitchen, where I am expected to pour fresh water into one side of his dish and cat food into the other. At that time I am free and he is happy. Not before.

Baines just doesn't get it.

That night I didn't take time to explain it to him. And I ignored Nigel. I just grabbed the telephone and dialed 911.

When the line was picked up, I told the sergeant on duty I wanted to report child abuse. Before I could say anything more, I was being transferred.

"Child Services Hotline."

"Oh. Hello. I need to report…a case of child abuse."

"What is your name, please, ma'am?"

"*Benjamin* Derby."

"Address?"

"What difference does it make? I'm not the person who was hit."

"We need this for our records, Mr. Derby."

That was better. I gave her our address and telephone number.

"Now, the name of the person who is being abused?"

"Nigel! Stop that!"

"Pardon me?"

"Sorry. It's my cat. His name is Batista. I don't know his last name."

"Your cat?"

"No, the kid who was hit. Batista."

"Address?"

Terrific. "I don't know his address. His family doesn't have a home."

There was a pause on the line.

"How do you know he was abused?"

"I saw it, in a grocery store. I know him."

Another pause. Finally: "Mr. Derby, let me talk to my supervisor and we'll call you right back."

"Why?"

Silence. "Why?" I asked again.

"Mr. Derby, I believe you, and I believe you want to help someone. Correct me if I'm wrong, but how old are you?"

"Twelve. Who cares?"

"And you can't give us an address for the child or a last name or a telephone number, is that correct?"

"He doesn't *have* a telephone number. I told you. He's homeless. Nigel!"

"Mr. Derby, I promise I'll have someone call you."

"What's *your* name?"

"I'm sorry. We don't give out personal details like that."

"You promise?"

"What?"

"To call back?"

"I promise."

"How soon?"

There was a moment's silence on the line. "Within half an hour."

"Really?"

"Truly."

What could I do?

I hung up and lunged into the living room toward the wing chair. Nigel was already flying past me and up the stairs to hide.

I started pacing the floor. Baines paced beside me, bouncing impatiently on his pads, sending out silent, urgent signals: Please, please, please!

I put the leash on Baines's collar. There was time. We started down the front walk.

Santa Barbara is a California seaside town where there are a lot of very rich people who live in the hills, and a lot of other people who don't.

It's a pretty town set between mountains and the Pacific. Its weather is mild and pleasant. In winter it isn't cold so much as drippy. Fog and rain alternate with what is an ordinary schedule of misty clearing days. If you happen to be homeless and can get here, you won't freeze, and you don't need a lot of clothing. The beaches look smooth and comfortable for sleeping, although recently that's been outlawed.

Television discovered us not very long after a horde of homeless people did. Even I can remember a time when we didn't see men and women of all ages begging for change on every corner.

Last year the city council decided to crack down. Hundreds, maybe even thousands, of needy people were streaming into town, looking for handouts, sleeping wherever they dropped, taking over parks and parts of the beach as their own.

Suddenly we saw ourselves on the nightly news. Anchor-people narrated film clips of us, interviewed us, attended council meetings and asked opinions of voters. They made us seem mean-spirited and frightened.

Then our newspaper got on the bandwagon and started writing long profiles of people down on their luck. And also about people who didn't seem to have any sympathy toward the needy. Which, to our minds–my own, Eileen's, my dad's–didn't seem fair.

Aunt Eileen is a woman who speaks out for what she believes. In this case, she wrote it all down. And it got printed, in the *Santa Barbara News-Press*. She was very proud. Publicly she was modest. This is what it said.

To the Editors:
Your editorial about treatment of our city's homeless forces me to respond.
Santa Barbara is neither nasty nor selfish. It is tired. People do give to others. We do organize clinics and shelters. We set up soup-kitchens. At Christmas we collect extra food and clothing and toys to give away.

But nothing changes.

Our instinctive sympathy, charity, and good feelings evaporate with every passing day. There is no place where someone isn't in need. This works heavily on our consciences, of course. But no matter how generous people are, being generous all the time is exhausting and makes many people angry rather than sympathetic.

You who live and work here have, it seems to me, a duty along with the rest of us not only to try to assuage the anguish we see and know around us, but equally important to make our good work as public as our failings—to the networks, to other newspapers, to all concerned citizens.

Of course, time has passed since Aunt Eileen got all that off her chest. Problem is, nothing changed.

In fact, things keep getting worse.

Maybe there is a silent fax system among the homeless. Hey, someone says, Santa Barbara's O.K. It's got beaches and sunshine and free food. Come on down!

"Come on down!"

I pulled at Baines and swung him around and we ran back toward home.

Why hadn't I thought of that before?

chapter eleven

As we approached the house, I dropped Baines's leash, and he ran up the steps to dance merrily on the porch, eager for a nighttime treat.

The sound of his toenails on the wood must have alerted Aunt Eileen, home from work, because by the time I got to the bottom of the stairs, she was standing in the doorway, holding open the screen door.

"You've certainly become popular in your old age," she said. "The phone hasn't stopped ringing since I got in."

She withdrew into the front hallway, and I followed, knowing that one of the calls would have been Felix's. I also knew that I had something more important to attend to.

"Felix, of course," Aunt Eileen told me, turning at a hall table we have where we leave messages and notes for each other. She picked up a notepad. "A Jennie Johnson called."

I looked at the floor.

"And some woman from a welfare agency."

"Welfare?"

"Well, no," Eileen corrected. "Child Protective Services."

She looked straight into my eyes. Her own were wide open but between them, just above her brow, was a warning line–a straight up-and-down wrinkle that usually means trouble. "Have you got something on your mind, Ben? I mean, do you feel mistreated?"

"No," I said quickly. "That's something else."

"Like what exactly?"

"It's hard to explain."

"Come into the kitchen and explain it to me, anyway," Eileen commanded.

I did.

"You mean the woman didn't believe you?" Eileen asked.

"I don't think so. I couldn't be definite, you see. I didn't have a lot of real information, only what I had seen."

"That should certainly be enough," Eileen declared. "You go dial that number and let me speak to her first."

I went across the kitchen and lifted the receiver off the wall phone there. I looked at the piece of paper she had handed me, and dialed. I turned to give the phone to Eileen and stopped with my hand in midair. She was regarding me with the same direct squint my dad used, the one even my grandmother shot at me when I least expected it. What did these people imagine I could grasp? What did they want me to understand without words?

She stood waiting, one hand on a hip, sort of bouncing in place. Then she grabbed the receiver from me.

"Hello?" Eileen said sharply. "Who is this speaking?" she paused. "Carol who?"

Eileen shook her head. "No, that's all right. I understand perfectly. We all protect one another, don't we? Now, I'm Benjamin Derby's aunt. He called you about a child he'd seen beaten in a grocery store." Pause. "Yes, I'm sure you did. Well, I just want you to know that Ben never lies. That's for starters.

And secondly, if he says this child was beaten, he's serious. You should take it seriously, and do something about it." Pause.

I looked at Eileen as she spoke. She's older than my dad by about three years. She still has a good figure. And she's pretty in her way when she relaxes, which isn't often.

Eileen's voice softened a tad. "Well, I just wanted you to know Ben is the kind of boy who cares." Pause. "No, I can't. But I'll let you speak to Ben. I'm sure he can."

Eileen passed the receiver to me. "Hello?" I was a little nervous.

"Hi, Ben. I'm Carol, and I'm an emergency caseworker with the CPS. I'm a mother with two children of my own, so I want you to know I do take this seriously. I'm glad your aunt feels so confident about you. I'm sure I will, too, after we've talked a bit."

I nodded. What a dumb thing to do into a telephone!

"I'm afraid we need more information than what you gave us earlier, in order to follow this up."

"There's not too much more I can give you. You see, Batista is homeless. Well, maybe he's got a roof over his head *somewhere*, but he's in the program at Sidewalk's End, so that must mean he qualifies. You know what I mean?"

"I do, and that's already more than we knew before. I know Lou Denton very well."

Oh! "Hey, that's terrific!" I said. "Because that's just what I was thinking about. You could go down to the center and get Batista's last name and his address and then go rescue him."

I could hear the smile in Carol's voice. "Well, not quite as fast as all that, but at least now we know how to go about locating him and his family."

"What do you mean, not as fast as that? The kid was really punched. I mean, he was flying through the air!"

"Well, Ben, I'm sure what you say you saw is true. But the

term 'abuse' is complicated. We can't just walk into someone's home and pick up a child and take him away from his family."

"Then what's the point of what you do?"

"Don't get discouraged, Ben. Remember, this is a serious charge. We have to investigate it. One witness of one incident isn't justification for the kind of action you want me to take."

"It's not me I worry about. It's Batista."

"I understand that. And I'll be at Sidewalk's End first thing in the morning to examine him."

"But what about tonight? Who knows what can happen tonight?"

"No one. I know how concerned you are, Ben, and I appreciate that. But there are only certain steps we can take, one by one. And the first is a physical examination. If anything more happens to your friend, we'll see it in the morning."

"Sure. If he's alive."

"Now, Ben, believe me. He'll be fine."

"Why, because he bounces off walls?"

"People calm down, Ben. Really. If his mother struck out, as you say, she feels better and guilty, both. Batista will survive."

"She has it 'out of her system'?"

"Exactly. Usually that's true. I'll see you in the morning. Oh, and Ben—I'm glad you called us. Really. We'll do everything we can."

I put the receiver back into its slot on the wall. "I think I'll call Felix."

I left Aunt Eileen in the kitchen and went into my dad's study. I sat behind his big desk and thought about putting Felix on the speakerphone. I didn't. You never know what he's going to say.

"*¡Hola!*"

"Felix, it's me."

"Benny, you wouldn't believe the people down there!"

"At Catholic Charities?"

"Those old guys really know the system." Felix's voice was full of surprise and admiration. Strange. "I mean, they go from one place to the next, knocking up people for food or cigarettes or a bed. Sometimes they even work. But they don't seem very anxious to change. You know what I mean? They like being on the street!"

"That's crazy."

"Yeah, well, I agree. But that's the way it is. Oh, these guys make all the right noises. They agree to everything and make promises. But you can just tell most of them are going to wander off happy the minute they get something in their bellies."

I wasn't convinced, but I didn't say so. I mean, Buster wasn't going to cease being a rat just because he was well-fed.

"Of course," Felix added quickly, "if they've got families with them, it's a bit different. Then they're more serious. But the older guys, hey, they got the whole thing bagged!"

"What about the people you work with? Don't they see the same thing you do?"

"Yeah, I think they do, some of them. But nobody's judging anyone else. That's cool. I mean, if someone wants to live rough, why not let them? But you still don't let them starve or be sick."

I thought a minute. "Maybe you're right. There's a guy at Sidewalk's End who told me there are certain rules, that the best way to survive is to understand how the system works. Being homeless isn't as simple as it sounds."

"You couldn't tell it by the guys I saw down there today. One thing. The workers there are really with it. And the woman who runs things–well, maybe not runs the place exactly but a lot of it, the woman I report to–she's amazing."

"How?"

"I've got to tell you, Benny, that if I ran into these guys day after day, it would wear me out. Because no one seems to change. Still, she's always smiling and hopeful and cheerful. It's unreal."

I thought of Lou Denton. "I know what you mean."

I was just about to tell Felix what I'd seen in the bodega and about the woman on the telephone, Carol, when he knocked that right out of my mind.

"You going to call Jennie?"

Wait a minute! "What do you mean?"

"I saw her on the way home."

Oh. "Maybe. A little later."

"I would, Benny. She's a fox!"

In a way I was tempted to call Jennie. I wanted someone to say, "Oh, gosh, Ben, that's awful!" and Jennie would have.

I hear people say girls "mature faster" than boys. They're smarter about "things" than we are.

Not that boys don't *talk* about "it."

But there's a lot of other stuff going on in seventh grade. There are new kids and rules and teachers and sports to sort out.

Girls must do that quicker than boys, too—sort things out. Because after five minutes, the next thing on their minds is finding the right boy to hang with.

I like Jennie Johnson. And I'm glad she likes me. So I'm not ready to kiss her off.

But I didn't call her.

Eileen and I had dinner—tuna salads, since I hadn't brought home the spaghetti sauce. Then I went upstairs fairly early, a little edgy about what would happen the next day at Sidewalk's End, about what Carol would find when she examined Batista.

I wanted to believe that nothing more terrible would have happened overnight. But deep down I couldn't.

It took me a long time to get to sleep.

I rolled out of bed at six, showered and dressed, and rushed downstairs to the kitchen. I needed breakfast, of course, but I had also decided I wanted something a little more nourishing at lunch than cheese sandwiches. I convinced myself that if I didn't eat what Sidewalk's End supplied, I'd be saving the place money.

The smell of the coffee Aunt Eileen measured every night to brew automatically the next morning filled the room. I was stuffing a couple of pieces of fruit into a brown paper bag when my dad shuffled sleepily into the room. I was surprised. He usually stays at the restaurant until late each night and doesn't make an appearance until long after the morning rush hour has passed.

He grinned at me groggily, then reached into a cupboard and drew down a gigantic coffee mug which he filled to its top. "So?" he said.

"So."

"Eileen told me about your situation when I came in last night. Anything I can do to help?"

I shook my head. "I don't think so. I mean, it's not my situation, anyway. It's this poor little kid's. All I want to do is make sure he survives."

My dad nodded and then turned to look out the kitchen window. He turned back. There! The squint. A long pause. Then: "You did the right thing," he judged. "We never know what we're getting into, do we?"

I shrugged.

"It sounded easy, I know. Hanging around with a bunch of little kids."

"It isn't *hard*," I said. "Besides, it's kind of fun."

"I think your teacher had a good idea, Ben. We all need to have our eyes opened from time to time. And what happened yesterday, what you saw and reported, doesn't happen just to people who are temporarily down on their luck." He ducked his head suddenly and lifted his mug, staring down into its bowl. "It can happen in the best of families."

I had a sudden sense that something important was about to happen. I didn't want it to.

But then Dad grinned up at me. "If you need backup, old sox, have whoever call me at work. I'm behind you a hundred percent."

"Thanks, Dad."

"Do a good job and keep your eyes open."

"I will."

He put down his mug and retied the belt to his bathrobe. I picked up my brown bag.

"Why don't you come by when you're finished, Ben. I'd be interested to know how things develop."

"O.K."

"Better hustle."

I moved toward the hallway. "See you."

"See you."

chapter twelve

It's an easy ride down into town from our house. Early in the morning, it's also educational. That's really the wrong word, I guess, but every time I rode down to Sidewalk's End that week, I noticed stores and shops I'd never seen before: new bookstores, new sports stores, new coffee places.

I bet Santa Barbara drinks more coffee than any other place in the world, fancy kinds and mixes. People stop in and order, and then take time to sit out on the sidewalk or a patio and drink and talk with their friends or read. Eileen says this is "very European," which means it pleases her.

I got to Sidewalk's End a little later than the day before. Lou Denton was already in her office and Debbie was helping Freida in the kitchen. Frank, too, was around, standing in a far corner, talking in low tones to some other Hispanic guy, very serious.

"Ben?"

Ms. Denton had seen me pass her door.

"Yes?"

"I got a call last night from Child Protective Services."

I nodded. No point in playing dumb.

"You want to tell me about what you saw?"

"Just what I told them. Batista was creamed, flying through the air. I called them but I couldn't tell them what they needed to know."

Ms. Denton nodded and smiled. "I'm pleased you took your responsibility seriously, Ben. We'll examine Batista when he comes in this morning."

"You think he'll show up?"

Ms. Denton nodded. "And when he does, we'll know what to look for."

"Like what?"

"It's fairly simple. We'll examine him for evidence of other incidents. Bruises, cuts, bumps."

"And if you find any?"

"Then we'll have to speak with his family."

"Is that all?"

Ms. Denton smiled at my question. "It's not all, Ben. It's the way these things begin. There are certain steps, certain procedures we have to follow. Carol probably told you that."

I didn't answer because just then LaKesha arrived with her father, and Wendell was not far behind, with his. Day Two was off and running.

I was more confident and more edgy, both, that day. Happier because I knew the kids a little, and thought I knew what to expect from most of them. Edgy because I kept looking at my watch, waiting for Carol whatever-her-name-was to show up.

Batista arrived after eight. I didn't see him come in because my back was to the doors and we were all sitting at the big table having breakfast. He sat down quietly across from me and reached out a pudgy hand for the toast plate. I looked over at him. I couldn't see any change from the day before. He didn't look tired. I didn't notice any strange marks. He seemed, well, normal.

"Ben?"

I turned around. Lou Denton was standing in the hallway beside a fairly stout woman with dark hair and gigantic glasses. She signalled for me to get up and join them. I did.

"This is Carol, the woman you spoke with last night," Ms. Denton said.

Carol stuck out her hand. "Hi, Ben. I told you I'd be here early. Now we can sort things out."

"Good," I replied. I liked the idea that I was involved in all this.

"Why don't you get Batista, Ben? We'll talk with him in the babies' changing room."

I turned around and walked back to the table. Batista's little hand fit right into mine and he didn't drag or even wonder where I was leading him.

"Thanks, Ben," Ms. Denton said, accepting the relay hand-off. "We'll take it from here."

"But—"

"This will take just a few minutes," Carol explained as Ms. Denton closed the door in my face.

For the next half hour I played with, and counted, and built, and picked up. I touched Stephanie's thin hair once. I pulled apart Miguel and Esteban. I stared at Buster in his cage across the room, watching his sharp pointed ugly little teeth savaging paper and new lettuce leaves. And I figured out why the four-year-old Barbara irritated me.

I had been trying to do what Ms. Denton said could be done so easily, deflect. Barbara and LaKesha were pulling apart a large picture book, its pages all but ready to pop from its binding. "Look, kids," I said as reasonably as I could, kneeling down before them and adding my fingers to theirs, "this is going to ruin what you both want. Why don't we see if we can find another book, one just as good and pretty, for one of you."

"For LaKesha," Barbara decided, tightening her grip.

LaKesha just stood there looking at me, little tears beginning to form in her huge brown eyes.

"But Barbara," I said, "you're older and more mature. There's plenty of time each day to read. Why not let LaKesha just look through it for a few minutes? I'm sure she'll give it to you soon."

"She doesn't even know how to read," Barbara announced.

LaKesha denied this. "Yes I do!"

Actually, she didn't.

"Besides," Barbara went on, "this book isn't for her. She's never even seen a horse."

"Yes I have!"

I was getting nowhere.

"Barbara, let's try to be understanding. You already know what's in the book, don't you?"

"Yes."

"Then let's give it to LaKesha for a while so that she won't want to read it again later. That way you'll have it back soon and she'll be finished with it."

After a second, Barbara's fingers loosened and she pulled away. "I wouldn't want to read it anyway, after *she* has!" she said, turning and stalking off into a corner.

Now, I wouldn't exactly say this was prejudice. It sounded like it to me, but maybe I was just a little too fast to imagine that. What really got me, though, was that what Barbara said was the kind of thing grown-ups say in anger. For a four-year-old, she had sure picked up a lot of attitude from somebody.

Just then I became conscious of someone running past my elbow. Batista.

I stood up quickly and looked back to see Ms. Denton and Carol standing in the hallway, watching him. I edged and backed slowly toward where they were, and then I turned around to face them directly. "So?" I asked under my breath.

Carol smiled. Everybody in this business always smiled!

"What did you find?" I persisted.

Carol kept smiling. "There was a scratch on Batista's right knee," she said. "But that's not much to go on, Ben. He could have fallen on a playground or on a sidewalk."

"He always wears jeans," I argued.

"Well, *here* he does," Ms. Denton said.

I was determined. "But what did he say? Did you ask him about last night?"

Carol nodded pleasantly. "He says his mother didn't hit him."

"What?! I saw her!"

"He says his mother doesn't hit him or his sisters, either."

"He doesn't *talk*!"

"Batista's English is only beginning to grow, Ben, but his Spanish is clear," Ms. Denton said evenly. "He can understand is what I mean. And he can nod."

"I saw that kid hanging in midair and crashing," I argued. "How do you explain that?"

"We can't," Carol told me. "But whatever happened, it hasn't disturbed Batista." She smiled again and gave a tiny shrug. "We'll just have to keep our eyes open, Ben, and wait."

"Wait for what?" I knew, but I didn't want to say the words out loud. I didn't even want to hear them in my mind.

"We'll stay alert, Ben," Carol said, hoisting her shoulder bag into place. "And I know you will, too."

Carol patted Ms. Denton's shoulder and started toward the front door.

Ms. Denton patted my shoulder and turned back toward her office.

I wanted to slug somebody.

"Who was that guy here this morning?" I asked Frank after lunch.

"He's from the county. Jorgé Geraldo. Without him, half these kids would be on the streets."

"Why? What does he do?"

Frank smiled. Not him, too! "He goes around to all the agencies, the places for homeless people. He listens and counsels and advises. He tells them about Sidewalk's End, among other things. He tells them about how to get their kids into school, or to medical services, or even something as simple as where to get a shower."

This was interesting. "So he'd know about all these kids' families and where—where they live?"

Frank nodded. "I can read your mind, *cholo*."

I blushed. "What?"

"Batista," he said simply. "It won't work. Jorgé is very sharp, very quiet. That's how he succeeds so well at getting people to trust him." He paused. "He would never give out information like that to you."

"But I'm on his side!"

Frank nodded. "I know that and you do. Still, there are some things that are always best kept confidential."

"I'm trying to help!"

Frank put his hand on my shoulder and stared, without smiling, into my eyes. "Straight talk?"

I nodded.

"You're a kid, Ben. You're not part of the system. Sometimes the system doesn't work. Sometimes it does. But it can't if people—no matter how well-meaning—screw it up."

"That's not fair! I'm not trying to screw anything up. I'm trying to get one little kid out of danger."

"That's what we all try to do, one by one, each of us," Frank said. "But Ben, you don't get it. You're too new, too young, and likely to do something that, in the end, might do more harm than good."

"I don't believe that."

"You don't have to. But it's true. Remember what you're doing here, kid. You're here to help all these children, not just one."

"I know that!" I snapped, pulling away from his hand. "But sometimes a new person sees what others can't. And I can see that Batista is right on the edge of getting lost in your wonderful system. Being hurt, maybe permanently. No one should stand by and watch that happen, not even a kid!"

chapter thirteen

It was amazing how quickly the day passed. Naptime–I sat with LaKesha, feeling that she deserved a little extra attention and affection since Barbara had been so rotten–and snack time and outdoor playtime.

I watched the clock carefully. I wanted to be near the front door at five-thirty so that when Batista's mother picked him up, I could jump on my bike right afterward and follow them.

That was my plan. Simple, easy to remember, foolproof.

When you've got flocks of little kids swirling around you screaming and shouting and arguing and laughing and crying, sometimes all at once, it's easy to get distracted.

By the time I realized that Batista had disappeared, it was too late to try to track him down. I had no idea in which direction he'd gone or where any of the various places homeless people spent each night were.

I was really down on myself when finally I did get on my bike and start north toward town. I remembered my dad telling me to stop in. He was the kind of guy who always made you feel better for talking, no matter what. I needed that.

I skidded to a stop on the sidewalk near Dad's restaurant. *She* was standing just behind a bus stop bench, her ankles crossed, leaning against the adobe wall that surrounded the restaurant's garden. I knew where she lived. No bus that came *down* State Street would take her anywhere near. She pushed off when she saw me. "Hi, Ben."

I got off my bike and leaned it against a wall just inside the front door of the restaurant. I looked back at her and then thought, Hey, why not? "Want to come in?" I asked. "Have a Coke or something?"

"Sure."

Jennie Johnson's not a bad-looking girl. She has very fair coloring and light brown hair that's curly. Her eyes are kind of green, kind of blue. Maybe they change with the light. And, unlike a few other girls in our class, she isn't tough. Some girls are competitive. Some girls want you to know right away that they're as good and as smart as you are.

Jennie's not like that. She may have good ideas and know things, but she doesn't hit you over the head with it.

We sat on barstools and I felt sort of good. I asked the bartender for our drinks and then swivelled a little to look at her more directly. "How's it going?"

She smiled softly. This smile I liked. "I'm learning a lot."

I nodded, but only to cover the fact that I was drawing a blank. I couldn't remember what agency she had chosen to work for during spring break. She must have guessed. "The hospice is a strange place."

Snap! "That's where Teddy works, too, isn't it?"

Jennie nodded. "Yes. And you know, Ben, he's amazing."

"What do you mean?"

"Well, I hate to admit it but I was a little frightened when I got there. I mean, someone my age isn't supposed to look at death like that, 'up close and personal.'" She smiled at her own words.

"Well, it's got to be scary," I said, feeling very wise.

"It is. But not to Teddy Hines. Ben, he is so gentle with those people, so giving."

I raised my eyebrows. "But you are too, probably."

"I needed to learn. I still need to learn. Somehow, Teddy just knows. It's amazing, the things he does, the things he thinks of to make people feel better."

"He's a strange kid."

Jennie nodded. "When we finish up, he just evaporates, disappears into thin air." She smiled nicely again. "'Who *was* that masked man?'"

"I know what you mean. When we get out of school, he heads in one direction on Monday, and another on Tuesday. It's mysterious. And he never calls any of us."

"Maybe he has a big family to look after."

"Maybe."

"Hi, kids!"

"Hi, Dad."

"Don't tell me," Dad said, his hand reaching out toward Jennie's shoulder. "This is Jennie."

Jennie blushed.

"Are you going to stay for dinner?" Dad asked.

"Oh, I couldn't," Jennie said, starting to slip sideways off her stool. "I should be getting home. Really."

"You're sure you wouldn't like to stay?" Dad suggested. "You could phone your family. I could have someone drive you both home later."

"No, thank you, Mr. Derby." Jennie looked like she was going to curtsy.

"Well, come on by any time you like, Jennie," Dad invited. "Drinks on the house."

Jennie smiled sort of weakly and disappeared.

"She's pretty, Ben."

I nodded.

"You want to stay for dinner?"

"No, Dad. I better get back for Baines and Nigel."

"Anything you want to tell me about your day?"

"Not much. I guess it's too soon to know what's going to happen. The boy showed up, and he was examined. But no one saw anything strange."

"Well, then, that made you feel better."

"It should have, maybe. What it does is worry me more." Dad put his hand on my shoulder and was about to say something, but I hadn't finished. "Not that I can't handle this. I just need to figure out how."

"I know you will, kiddo. I have faith." Dad clapped my shoulder. I looked up at him. *That* squint was forming, his eyes just barely beginning to narrow. I guess he changed his mind. "Stay loose, Ben."

I grinned, relieved. "See you."

"See you."

I backed away from the bar and reached out for my bike.

I *did* feel better.

The thing about having a sheltie and an orange tabby is that when they shed, you can't tell who's to blame. There's orange and white and light brown hair over everything. You learn to live with this and ignore it. Unless, as I do when I greet Nigel each night, you get down on all fours to snuffle along at carpet level. Then it's sneeze, sneeze, and uck! picking long hair out of the corners of your mouth.

I read somewhere that having pets helps reduce stress and

pressure, that a dog or a cat—*anything* to worry over—may even keep you alive longer, because then you don't worry so much about yourself.

Nigel and Baines didn't live up to this advertising. But I wasn't worrying about myself. It was Batista I worried about.

Felix pulled me out of my funk. "Come on over for dinner," he invited. "Mom's doing something English."

I smiled. Felix's mom, Irene, is my dad's bookkeeper, and has worked for him ever since he opened the restaurant. But she hates Mexican food. There are three reasons I can think of: first, working at the restaurant means she can't help but smell that part of Dad's menu all day. Secondly, she probably eats it every day at noon. Thirdly, she's been eating it all her life.

At home, Irene wants something else, something different, anything different. She is a good cook, and a happy woman—at least around me. Felix warns me she has a temper that could flatten a house. I never see it. I think Felix is probably bragging, just as he does when he talks about what his brother and three sisters are doing. A lot of what Felix says always sounds too good to be true.

Anyway, whenever Irene cooked new kinds of food, I wanted to be there. There were a lot of things I had never had except at her house—Polynesian food, Indian food—Indian from Asia, not American Indian. Sushi I had there for the first time. Hungarian goulash and lots of different pasta with unusual toppings. And for dessert—napoleons, English trifle, wild fruit like kiwi and dates and figs and mangoes and passion fruit.

I wrote a short note to Aunt Eileen, gave Baines a five-minute relief session, and bicycled down the hill, turning west on Arrellaga and getting to Felix's house in about ten minutes.

What I smelled as he opened the door didn't seem all that strange: onions. I guessed they were just part of whatever new taste-sensation Irene was working on.

"So, how's it going?" Felix asked as we ambled into his den and sank down on a couch to stare at the television screen.

"Problems."

"Yeah? What kind?" Felix is always happy to hear about problems because he feels so sure he can solve them.

I told him about Batista and the Child Protective Services.

"You mean they're not doing anything?" Felix's voice rose.

I shook my head. "They don't have enough evidence."

"Bananas! What do they need?"

I shrugged. "Witnesses probably."

"Well, that's easy," Felix said quickly. "I'll just phone them up and say I saw the same thing."

"Won't do."

"Why?"

"Because you're just a kid, like me."

"I'll disguise my voice."

I laughed.

"Well, then, we'll set up a stakeout."

"I thought about that. But I don't know where his family lives."

"It can't be too hard to figure out. There are only so many places they could be, and they've all got to be within a certain distance of where you're working. You know what, Benny? I bet there's a map where *I* work. I'm sure there is. The kind of thing you hand out to people in need, telling them where soup kitchens are and bathrooms and shelters and all."

"Really? Could you get one?"

"Sure. Then we could do a process-of-elimination thing, you know, or even just go around and look in at them all."

"They let the public in?"

"Why not? The public's paying. Or at least some of the public. Catholic Charities is always raising funds, and who else but members of the public comes across?"

"I never thought of it."

"I bet the same thing happens where you are."

"Probably."

"Boys?"

Irene was ready. Her English menu was fairly simple: what she called "bangers and mash," which is English sausages atop a mound of mashed potatoes with fried onions scattered all over the plate.

"We can meet at the end of the day," Felix told me, getting up and stretching on the way to the kitchen. "We can probably hit half a dozen places before it gets dark."

"Then what?"

Felix grinned. "Simple. Then we high-jack the kid."

chapter fourteen

The next morning Batista didn't come to school.

I didn't panic. What I thought was, Well, of course. He told his mother about Carol and Ms. Denton and their questions, and she got angry enough to keep him home.

Following that sane thought came the other: she beat the hell out of him. After all, if he hadn't done whatever it was that was so awful on Monday, no one would be snooping around now.

Ms. Denton seemed as concerned as I was. "Maybe he has a cold," she said to me around nine o'clock. "We don't allow children in school who are sick, you know. It's too great a risk to the others."

"Could you call?" I asked.

She shook her head. "It's not just that they haven't a phone, Ben. But shelters close up at seven-thirty each morning."

"They do?" That meant Batista couldn't have been kept "home."

Lou Denton smiled as though what she were going to say she had said many times before. "That's why you see people on the street with everything they own in a shopping cart or a large plastic trash bag. Shelters can't provide space enough to leave your worldly possessions in storage. And they haven't enough staff, most of them, to stay open all day to protect them. So everyone is, well, herded out onto the street in the morning and then let back in around five-thirty."

"Even small children?"

"Even small children. Which is why it's so hard to break the pattern of homelessness. How can a parent go for an interview or job-training if he or she has to worry who will take care of his child at the same time?"

"So they just wander around, hang out?"

"Yes. At the beach, in parks, at facilities that are open during the day for distribution of food or clothing."

"Like Catholic Charities?"

"Exactly. Their offices *close* in the evenings."

Ms. Denton frowned, a first! "I do worry, you know," she admitted.

I did, too, as the day wore on. But Felix and I had agreed to meet at six on the corner of Garden and de la Guerra to start our research. So no matter what happened during the day, or didn't, I felt just as confident as Sherlock Holmes. There wasn't anything that couldn't be solved if you were smart enough.

At about ten o'clock, a blonde woman, maybe thirty and very round, arrived at Sidewalk's End carrying two big shopping bags. The children seemed to recognize her, and all together they rushed toward one end of the large play area as she set up what was to be a puppet stage.

"What's this all about?" I asked Debbie, who stood near me watching, a smile on her lips and her arms folded across her chest.

"It's part two of what we had last week," she said quietly. "It's a way to teach kids not only to try to understand their parents, but also to try to understand themselves."

"Heavy."

Debbie's smile broadened. "Not really. The topic is heavy but the treatment is light. I mean, if I told you I was going to tell you how parents sometimes went around the bend, crashed, got angry or impatient or even violent, you'd probably choose not to attend the lecture. But if I showed you all this with hand puppets, chances are you wouldn't mind a bit."

I grinned a little myself. "You mean if I had fun, I wouldn't fight learning?"

"Exactly."

We watched as the puppeteer pulled first props and then the puppets themselves from her boxes. The kids were already enchanted. "Where's Papa Bear?" one of them shouted. "Where's Mama Bear?" came from someone else.

Ms. Denton stepped forward and took a position to the right of the improvised stage, at the foot of which sat, knelt, stood, bounced, or jiggled our daily population. "You all remember Judy from last week."

A chorus of agreement rang. Judy stood modestly waiting, dressed like one of her puppets–full skirt with lots of pockets, cardigan sweater, and a barrette holding her hair back off her forehead. "Well, this week she's come back to show us more puppets and to tell us a different story."

"Where's Papa Bear?" shouted Max.

"Papa Bear is out today," answered Judy. "We have new friends this week."

She put a puppet on one hand and then slid her fingers into another. "This is Cody Bear, and this is Baby Bear. And this is Pockets. Why do we call her Pockets?"

Barbara's hand shot up. "Because she has pockets in her apron!"

"Good for you." Judy nodded encouragingly.

"I don't get it," I whispered to Debbie.

"You will," she whispered back.

"Now," Judy began, "one day Baby Bear went to school. But he was feeling sad. Why do you think he would be feeling sad?"

"Because he had to go to school!" Max shouted.

"That could be one reason. What else would make Baby Bear sad?"

"He had to leave his mother," Barbara guessed.

Judy nodded. "That could be true. Anyone have another idea?"

"He didn't like his teachers?" asked Wendell.

Judy smiled. "Maybe. There are lots of reasons why sometimes we feel sad, aren't there? So Baby Bear was feeling sad and gloomy, and when he got to school the other boy bears in his class, like Cody, made fun of him."

"Because he lost his dad," Max supplied.

"Because his lunch was awful," Wendell added.

"Because his mother had gone away," Barbara suggested softly.

"Well, what would you do if someone laughed at you and hurt your feelings?" Judy asked, moving her fingers in Baby Bear's body to bring his hands up to his eyes.

"Hit him!" Wendell.

"Tell my dad." Max.

"Run home and tell my grandmother on him." Barbara.

"Right!" Judy made Baby Bear nod his head in agreement. "What you'd do is tell someone, talk about what had made you unhappy. And that's what we all need to do, isn't it? Find someone we can tell our secret hurts to."

"What was the program last week?" I whispered to Debbie.

"How to understand an adult's anger," she said under her breath. "How to tell when your mother or father is angry at you, or really angry at something else."

"What's the point of that?"

Debbie smiled softly. "Well, Ben, it covers a lot of territory. Sometimes anger comes out as drinking, or violence, or shouting. A child needs to understand how much of that he's responsible for, and how much has nothing to do with him personally. Actually, it's armor against life."

That made a certain amount of sense. Still... "How much of that can a kid get? I mean, it sounds kind of hazy."

"It's subtle, Ben. But what Judy tries to do is alert kids so they can be on the lookout and protect themselves. Barbara, for instance."

"What about her?"

"She's just been taken from her mother for maybe the third time this year. Her mother drinks and she's angry, of course, disappointed, down, ready to blame herself and anyone within range for whatever problems she has. Barbara can learn to understand the difference between her mother being angry at her, and her mother's anger at the world. And if she can see the difference, she's going to feel better about herself. See?"

I nodded.

"So," Judy asked the crowd of tiny fans in front of her, "who do you think we should go to to share our feelings?"

"Your dad!" Max.

"Your mother!" Barbara.

"Nobody." Wendell.

Some of the younger kids had other suggestions but not the words to do more than shout or giggle or, if they really could get the words out, to focus on something entirely different—like Pockets's pockets ("What's in them?"), Cody's blue jeans ("Just the same as mine."), hunger ("When do we get lunch?"). Some of this was in English, some in Spanish.

The program only lasted maybe fifteen minutes and led, naturally enough, to the idea that *one* person a kid could talk to would be a teacher.

There was time after this to go outside to play in the yard before lunch. I was surprised when we got there. There were two people I'd never seen before standing waiting for us. But if I was in the dark, they weren't. One of them, a large man about my dad's age with a fat black face and shiny strong arms showing out of a T-shirt, came up to me right away. "Hi, Ben. I'm Doug Bailey."

I shook his hand.

"I'm glad we have an extra pair of hands around. Have you met Betty Mendoza?"

He turned halfway and motioned a really beautiful woman forward. She quickly stepped on a cigarette and then smiled bashfully at me. "Hi, Ben."

"So who are they?" I whispered to Frank the first chance I had.

"Volunteers. Doug's a policeman. He comes two or three times a week, whenever he's off. Mrs. Mendoza lives not very far away from here and has half a dozen kids of her own."

"Oh," I said, bending down to pick Miguel up off the gravel, and setting him upright.

Then two things hit me, hard. (1) A policeman! (2) Felix and I were planning a kidnapping!

I don't know why I hadn't seen things so clearly before.

Yes, I do. Felix and I were so hot to rescue Batista from danger that we never even considered how what we wanted to do would look to the rest of the world.

After all, we were planning to grab him and get him to safety, not hold him for ransom or do him any harm.

I tried not to stare at Doug Bailey. I tried not to not stare. I pretended he was just another well-meaning private person who came to Sidewalk's End to help out. But it was hard.

He looked tough. Not that he didn't smile and wasn't gentle with the kids. He was. But he was big. And he was a policeman. I didn't have any trouble at all imagining him in uniform with a revolver strapped to his belt, or behind the wheel of his cruiser chasing Felix and me on our bikes, Batista tucked under one of my arms and screaming bloody murder. I mean, how would *he* know we were acting in his best interests?

It was not an easy day. We had six adults on hand–Ms. Denton and Debbie, Frank and myself, Doug Bailey and Mrs. Mendoza–for about thirteen kids. A good ratio, and necessary, because Ms. Denton decided we should all go to the zoo.

It wasn't a long trip and the kids were excited and well-behaved in the vans, fearing that something one of them did would change Ms. Denton's mind. Still, unless you're three, a zoo is a zoo is a zoo.

Naptime was a relief. I made a special effort to get close to Barbara. I still didn't like her much, but having heard about her outside life, I tried to be a little more caring. She allowed this, but by the time she closed her eyes and drifted off, I didn't feel I had made much of an impression.

I hung around Sidewalk's End until about ten to six, picking up things, helping to clean dishes, rearranging books or mats. Finally I leapt on my bike and pedalled like crazy to the appointed corner.

Felix wasn't alone. Teddy Hines was standing quietly maybe a foot away. Both of them stayed motionless as I slid to a stop. "What?" I asked.

"We're too late," Felix told me.

I went cold. "What do you mean?"

"The doors are closed."

"What doors?"

"Where your kid sleeps," Felix explained.

"He's at Mission Felicidad," Teddy added.

"He is? How do you know?"

"When Felix told me what you guys were doing, I remembered seeing Batista there."

"What were you doing there?" I asked suspiciously.

"Passing by," Teddy replied easily. "What made me look at him was he was in the backyard with a soccer ball. He was good. It made me smile."

"That's Batista," I agreed.

"He's a tough little kid. Besides, I'd seen him before, playing outside a hotel," Teddy added. "He took a fall on the cement there and bounced right back on his feet. He can concentrate. It's amazing."

"So," Felix broke in, waving some crumpled fliers in his right hand, "we don't even need these maps. We already have a target. Mission Felicidad. And Teddy says we can get in after five-thirty."

"How?"

"There's a back porch, where people go out to smoke," Teddy told us. "There's also a big iron gate that guards the yard."

"How high?" asked Felix.

"High," Teddy said. "But there's a gap between its posts big enough to slip through."

"Sure, and be seen by anybody who's on the porch."

"If they're watching," Teddy smiled.

"I don't get it," I admitted.

"Teddy will be inside!" Felix announced.

"He will?"

Teddy nodded. "I can get there before five-thirty, before

the doors close. They'll never notice just another kid following the crowd in. I can find somewhere to hide out until we're ready."

We're? sounded in my mind but I didn't let it out. Having looked at Doug Bailey all day, I wanted as much help as we could get.

"I can get people to look somewhere else when you're ready," Teddy went on. "Like a decoy."

"We wait till it's dark," Felix directed, "and then we slip in, grab the kid, and hustle out."

"O.K.," I said, "and then what do we do with him?"

"Take him to the cops." Felix had no doubt.

"Maybe get him to an adoption agency?" Teddy was less certain.

"You know this is kidnapping."

"Hey, *cholo*, whose idea was this to begin with?"

"Yours! Well, also mine, I admit. But if you look at it from the outside, what we're doing is pretty scary."

"So is being whomped up the side of the head day after day," Felix judged. I couldn't think of a smart answer for that.

"Let's go look the place over, case it," Felix suggested.

It was getting dark and cool. I was hungry. Baines needed his walk.

Mission Felicidad was exactly as Teddy had told us: the building itself wasn't much—flat-roofed, dirty-looking, not many windows or much light, at least visible to us on the street. There *was* a paved-over side area behind a chain fence that had a padlock on it. And, spying from across the street, we could see a few older guys sitting on the steps of the back stoop, or standing around its bottom, smoking and talking. We could also see the door behind them that would get us into the shelter itself.

"Are you sure Batista's in there?" I wondered.

Teddy nodded. Then, after a minute, he said, "He *was*. Maybe he's moved. Who knows?"

"Swell, so here we are searching for someone to save who hasn't waited for us to come get him."

"Hey, Benny, lighten up. The worst thing that happens is we get a look inside and leave. The best is that we grab him and get him to safety. I don't think those are such bad choices."

I shrugged.

"What time?" asked Teddy. "What time do you want to get in?"

I looked at Felix. As ever, he sounded very confident. "It gets dark around six-thirty," he calculated. "Let's say we'll be out here by seven-thirty, ready to slip in."

"Make it eight," Teddy advised. "Supper is served in the kitchen. It takes a while for kids to quiet down after that."

"Right," Felix agreed. "Eight sharp. I'll get my mom to ask Benny for dinner and then we can go outside to ride our bikes for a while. She'll never know."

Teddy nodded and smiled a little. Then he lifted a hand and started to walk away. "See you guys then," he said over his shoulder. "Eight sharp."

Felix and I stood across from the Mission Felicidad and watched Teddy as he turned a corner and disappeared from view. "Maybe Teddy's wrong," I said very quietly.

"About what?"

"That this is where Batista is."

Felix shook his head. "According to Teddy, there's probably only one other place where a whole family could stay."

"Where?"

"The Navarre."

"What's that?"

"A hotel, Benny. Sort of a welfare hotel."

"You mean that place down on Gutierrez?"

Felix nodded. "But I'd put my money on Teddy that he's here."

"Shouldn't we go check, just in case?"

Felix shrugged. "If you want to, sure. But it's a waste of time."

"I don't get it. What makes you think Teddy knows so much?"

"Geez, Benny, it's a good thing we're friends. I mean, if I weren't around, you'd be blindsided, you're so slow."

"What are you talking about?"

"Teddy," Felix said, swinging his leg over the bar of his bike and pedalling in place.

"What about him? All I asked was how does he know so much about all this, these places."

Felix was already pushing off toward the hotel. "Because, Benny Banana, he's a homeless kid, too."

chapter fifteen

"How do you know that?" I asked, pedalling furiously to keep up with Felix. "How do you know Teddy Hines is homeless?"

"You don't have to be a rocket scientist, Benny. Just figure it out."

I pumped hard. "Did he tell you?"

Felix shook his head. "Think about it."

We rode a moment as I did. Felix looked over at me quickly. "He ever phone you after school?"

"No."

"You ever see him in new clothes?"

"No."

"You ever hear him talk about his folks, or a brother or sister?"

"No."

"You know where he lives?"

"Of course I don't! Do you?"

"No, because he keeps moving," Felix said in a very patient, but also smug, tone of voice. "You ever see him with any money?"

"What do you mean?"

"At school. In the cafeteria."

I thought about it. "No."

"Come on, then, Benny. Put it together. Remember when we said good-bye to him the other day? He just turned and whipped right around toward the beach. I mean, hey, the sun's long gone."

"You think he sleeps on the beach?"

Felix turned left. I followed. "I bet he doesn't sleep in a house like us. I bet he doesn't have a house."

He skidded to a complete stop.

"Hey, I'm not putting him down," Felix added. "He just hasn't had the breaks, that's all."

"But he's so smart."

"Why not? That's not one of your homeless rules, I hope."

I felt rotten, slow and stupid and at the same time really sorry if what Felix said was true. I got off my bike. There were a thousand questions I needed to ask Teddy Hines. Did he have parents? How did he eat? Where did he sleep? How could he study? Was he even going to stay in Santa Barbara? Who looked after him when he was sick?

There wasn't a lot of time for mulling all this over, though, because Felix was a setter hot on the trail, pointing.

The Navarre Hotel isn't pretty. Santa Barbara has a lot of hotels and probably a hundred motels, all of which are in better shape than this place.

It's only a few yards off State Street, and you probably wouldn't notice it at all except for a banner that's hung over the front door: Low Rates: $35, Families Included.

The building itself is painted a sort of vomit-yellow, all cracked and peeling. It's only three stories high. On either side of its central doors are two big glass windows that haven't been washed in years.

Felix and I watched as some old man wove along the sidewalk ahead of us and then lurched to his left and managed to pull open the hotel door.

"This isn't going to be fun," Felix guessed, locking his bike and mine to a parking meter.

"It's not supposed to be fun," I reminded. "We're here on a mission."

Felix put his hands around his eyes and peered through the dirty hotel windows. Before I could come up beside him to do the same, he turned away and took my arm, shoving me back.

"We'll have to split up," he announced.

"Why?"

"Because you know what your little kid looks like and I don't, for one," Felix said. "And I'll have to cover for you at the front desk."

I frowned.

"Think about it," Felix commanded. "Besides, this isn't like an ordinary hotel."

"Why not?"

"You'll see."

Felix let go of my arm. He pulled open one of the two doors and stepped into the lobby. I followed.

Even though it was nearing darkness, it was still easy to see what Felix had meant. In most hotels you see a front desk where you get welcomed and sign in to get your key. In the Navarre, *welcome* didn't seem the right word: the desk clerk was standing behind a sort of stand which was enclosed on all four sides by wire caging for safety.

The lobby itself was unlike any other I had seen. On one wall was a bank of vending machines, for Cokes and snacks and shaving kits. In the middle of the place was a gigantic table on which were stacked copies of different fliers: Santa Barbara, welfare, Aid for Dependent Children, clinics, soup kitchens.

And where in most lobbies you see big comfortable chairs and couches, with lamps nearby for reading, in this one there wasn't a cozy piece of furniture anywhere. The whole place looked like a big dark barn, and the only light that was shining was the one that hung above the desk clerk's station.

I didn't have more time to scope out the place because Felix whispered at me, "Go!" and pointed to a stairway off to the right as he approached the desk clerk. I knew what he was doing but I wasn't convinced it was necessary. It was like something we saw on television. The desk clerk looked to *me* like he couldn't care less who came in or out. Still, I tried hard to get very small and invisible as I hung a quick turn and started to disappear up the staircase.

If you want to know, it was like a horror movie.

The walls didn't moan or drip blood, or swell in and out like a monster breathing; the stairs didn't scream, bats and birds weren't dive-bombing out of nowhere. But other than that, it was just as scary.

The first thing that happened was my nose puckered up, my nostrils got tight and tiny, and I started to breath through my mouth so I wouldn't inhale all the smells that circled around me as I climbed: cooking oil, stale pee, cigarette smoke, spilled beer.

I got to the top of the stairway and looked down a narrow dark hall with one window at its end. On both sides of the hallway were rooms with their doors opened, or partly so. I could hear television sets and radios, their volume levels high. I could hear men laughing and joking and swearing. I could hear babies crying. I could hear people snoring despite all this.

For a minute I didn't move. I looked to my right. I would have to make two tours, one of the second floor and one of the third. I decided that I might as well start at the top, so I climbed the other flight of stairs–breathing the same way–and came out looking down an identical hall with an identical window dirty and open onto the street below.

The first room into which I looked—and quickly because I was nervous—was empty. I was relieved. The second—I was moving down the hall along the right-hand wall—had bunk beds in it, and on the bottom was a pregnant woman, her stomach very big, lying on her back with a washcloth over her eyes. Bouncing above her were two little kids who looked about three. Neither of them was Batista.

I kept moving, trying to ignore all the odors that filtered out to me: sweat, rancid fast food, stopped-up plumbing. I couldn't imagine how any family would want to spend thirty-five dollars a night to stay here. If you added that up, it was a lot of money week by week for a real dump.

I peeked into the third room and saw two old guys seated on a bed with playing cards between them, bottles of beer scattered at their feet.

The fourth room was occupied by a very young man and a woman I thought older, and more kids: four. Maybe the very young man was the fifth and oldest. No one looked like Batista, and I was glad.

As I turned around near the window at the end of the hall, a furry little comet flashed across my vision at floor level. I didn't even have to think: one of Buster's cousins or pals. Get me out of here!

I tiptoed quickly back along the left wall, looking into every room for Batista and not finding him. I hit the top of the stairway and hurried down, feeling as though I were jumping out of a burning plane.

I started along the second floor hallway, again on the right, suddenly remembering that Wendell's parents were worried that if he got a really good nap at Sidewalk's End, he wouldn't be able to sleep where they lived. This was probably that place. This, or another place very much like it. I agreed with them.

Into each room I looked were people obviously ill or drunk or passed out. And there must have been fifteen or twenty kids all told. Nothing I saw gave me any hope for Batista, or Wendell for that matter. Everything made me more and more certain Batista was in danger.

"Yo, kid!"

I froze. Out of the gloom and murk of the room closest to the stairway lurched a huge, grizzled hulk—probably three hundred pounds of him, unshaven, with a beer-belly bigger than a pregnant elephant. Before I could get my feet to do their stuff, a gigantic paw grabbed my right shoulder and rooted me to the floor.

"You forgetting something, kid?"

I couldn't speak. My worst nightmare gripped my shoulder harder.

"Where's my beer? Where's my change?"

"Uhhh…"

"You owe me, kid. You better deliver."

He let go of me for a second, wavering in the doorway, getting his balance. I took a step out of his reach but he righted himself fast and grabbed me again.

"You got five minutes, understand? Five minutes to get back up here with my beer *and* my money. I ain't whistlin' Dixie, kid. Five minutes, five!"

He pushed me toward the staircase.

"Five minutes, boy. Or else!"

I was already on my way down to the lobby.

I didn't stop there. I waved at Felix as I ran for my life out onto the street.

I pumped back north on my bike, Felix at my side. I told

him about the guy and the beer. Naturally, Felix laughed, which didn't make me feel better or safer. All I wanted to do was get home, play with Baines and Nigel, and hide in bed. I didn't even want to *think* about what we had planned for the next day.

chapter sixteen

As it happened, I didn't have a lot of time to think about it. When I wheeled into our driveway I saw my grandmother's car parked there, a pale gray, ten-year-old Toyota station wagon still in great shape, shiny and always clean. I had forgotten about her weekly Wednesday visit and dinner.

My grandmother's not ancient, not really, and usually she's full of well-meant advice which I can handle. I don't always follow it, but once a week I can sit still with an attentive look on my face as it's delivered.

She looks a lot like Aunt Eileen, which I suppose isn't too surprising, with straight gray hair cut rather short and close to her face. She dresses well, as though there were always a chance she'd meet someone important when least expected.

Grandmother's greatest gift, I think, is her voice. Over the years it has deepened and softened. Even when she is angry its pitch does not rise. Her speech comes out faster, but always in the same low musical register. My father says this is because she still smokes five or ten cigarettes a day and always, always has what she calls a "dressing drink." A dressing drink is a cocktail she pours for herself at the end of the day as she "freshens up" before dinner. It doesn't matter whether she's going out. If she is, she likes to think that her arrival at a restaurant to meet friends, or at a party, is jollier because she's had a head start on the evening.

She was sitting alone in Dad's den behind his desk, her drink neatly atop a coaster sitting on Dad's blotter, when I closed the front door. "Well," she called, not yet seeing me or even knowing who had arrived, "at last!"

I edged around the den door frame and let myself be identified. Grandmother smiled. "Just the very person I was looking for!"

She says this every time she visits so I put the sentiment aside. "Hi, Grandma," I said.

She lifted her drink and toasted me silently before taking a sip from it. She put the glass down. "So, tell me, how's your class project going?"

"O.K."

"It's good to find out how other people live."

I nodded.

"Your father tells me you may be in over your head."

I didn't believe this. He might have told her about Sidewalk's End, but not that. Still, it was easier to go along. "Yeah?"

"Yes," she corrected firmly.

I shrugged.

"You know, Benjamin, we live in a peculiar country."

"We do?"

"We do," she echoed. "Everyone believes in individual freedom and responsibility. That's a good thing. Yet everyone also—at least most good people—wants to help his neighbors when there's trouble."

"What's so strange about that?"

"Nothing, dear. That, too, is part of being American. But

sometimes"—she took another sip—"sometimes, these two ideas clash."

She stood up from Dad's leather swivel chair and came toward me, her arm outstretched. Her hand snaked around my neck and she drew me farther into the room. She spoke at the same time as she forced us both to settle on the couch. "There are some problems Americans do not understand, you know."

"Like what?"

Grandma squinted at me; she was not more than three feet away, and she squinted—as though she were behind glass in a zoo, on the free side, that is, peering in, expecting me to read her mind or understand something she's not going to talk about but wants to. It's the exact same look I get from Aunt Eileen and Dad. Weird. Maybe it's a family thing. The Derby Squint. The Curse of the Derbys.

"Like poverty or disease or homelessness," she finally said. "Americans believe they can solve any puzzle. They believe that people can pull themselves up by their bootstraps if they want. They believe people can find a job if they want to, can care for their families if they love them. Ideally, all that is true."

I still couldn't see where this was headed.

"There are times when people in need actually require assistance. Their hearts are good, their intentions wonderful, but their abilities just aren't as great as a lot of us would have them."

The squint. And a few split seconds for me to get it. I didn't.

Grandma sighed, frustrated. "The problem we *all* face, Ben, is in drawing a line that separates good intentions from intrusion."

"What line?"

Another sip and her glass was empty. She leaned down to put it on the floor. "Remember when your father and Eileen chipped in to treat Grandfather and me to that wonderful trip all around the world?"

"Sort of." I couldn't have been more than two at the time, but over the years since I had certainly heard enough about it.

"Well, Ben, we saw things you wouldn't believe. We saw people living in conditions not only unimaginable but that stayed in your memory for years and years. Now, a lot of people don't want to visit India, for example, because the poverty there assaults them. They feel powerless before it. And they're right. They are powerless. The prudent traveler knows there isn't money enough in the world to help everyone there who needs it."

Where was Aunt Eileen?

"And prudent people here, in this country, know there isn't money enough to help all the homeless, all the addicted, all the lonely. Do you see what I'm driving at?"

"No, I don't," I said frankly.

Grandma patted my hand, "What I'm saying, Benjamin, is that to volunteer to try to help other people is necessary and good. But you have to be realistic about what you can expect to do."

Suddenly I did know where this chat was leading, and I didn't like it. "Did Dad ask you to tell me this?"

"No, not for a minute," Grandma said quickly. In a lower, almost regretful tone she added, more to herself than to me, "He never asks my help for anything." She sighed and straightened her back against the pillows on the sofa. "It's just something I think you should know. It will be helpful, dear. Later."

"You think I shouldn't worry about how other people treat their children?"

"I didn't say that, Ben. What I'm trying to say is that you must understand that your little boy's family is exactly that, *his* family. No matter how *you* feel, it is intrusive, nosy . . . not polite to try to tell someone how to raise a child who isn't yours."

"Look, all I'm trying to do is make sure Batista stays safe. That's all."

"Give me the benefit of the doubt, dear," Grandma said then. "Let's assume for a moment that what you saw didn't happen the way you think. Suppose what *did* happen was an accident of some kind. Now you've raised a hue and cry. The authorities are suddenly involved. They barge in, make accusations, disturb whatever harmony existed in that family. Suppose it turns out that you, and they, are wrong. Don't you think that would be unfair?"

"No, I don't." I stood up and positioned myself at the end of the couch, out of reach. "I think that if there's even a tiny chance Batista is being hurt, he deserves help."

"But—"

"And if I'm wrong, if someone else did this and was wrong, at least we would still be acting for good reasons. But, Grandma, I'm not wrong! I know what I saw and I know what it means!"

"Benjamin, *dear*, I believe you. I'm only trying to point out that people deserve privacy and consideration."

"No, what you're saying is what Felix says."

"What *does* Felix say?"

"That some of the people where he's volunteering actually like the way they live."

"Perhaps some of them do."

I shook my head. I also heard the front door being opened in the hallway. "You're telling me to look the other way, not to help. I don't get it, Grandma. If you see something that can be changed and made better, wouldn't *any* American want to try?"

My grandmother stood up. She, too, now could hear footsteps in the hall: Aunt Eileen's. For a second her lower lip trembled. I sensed she was right on the edge of breaking, but she got hold of herself. "You know what your father would say?"

"What?"

"Hi, you two!"

"He would tell you to pick your shots. To aim at those people or problems you had a real chance of solving. To conserve your energies, knowing there was only so much one person could do."

I shook my head. "You're wrong, Grandma. Dad agrees with *me*. He understands. And he's proud of what I'm doing."

I was steamed. Aunt Eileen stepped between us. "Mother, I need a drink and you're probably dying for a little refresher," she suggested, taking my grandmother and turning her away from me and starting to walk across the room to the second door that led into the kitchen.

It was late. I was starving. I turned in the opposite direction and grabbed Baines's leash.

chapter seventeen

To my relief, Doug Bailey was not in sight the next day. And Frank had classes, although later in the afternoon he would turn up. Mrs. Mendoza was there, and Debbie, Freida, Ms. Denton. And Batista.

I'd been a little slow getting out of the house, and by the time I arrived at Sidewalk's End, most of the kids—except Wendell—had already been delivered, Batista among them. So I never saw who it was who brought him or whether or not that person was nervous.

Batista wasn't. He was as bouncy as before, running across the play area and then sliding on his knees into a pile of building blocks. He made it to his feet, put the blocks back in a sort of random-order tower, and backed up slowly, aiming to do the whole act again. He did.

"Looks perfectly healthy to me," Ms. Denton said as I stood watching him.

I nodded. "Where was he yesterday? Did you ask him?"

Ms. Denton smiled easily. "With his mother. She had to go to the doctor and she took him with her."

"That's it?"

"What do you mean, Ben?" asked Ms. Denton. "What more do you want?"

I shrugged. Honestly, I didn't know what more I wanted. Yes, I did, too. I wanted to hear how horrible Batista's life was, how badly he was treated, how much he needed my help. Maybe I began to feel defensive. A whole raid, search-and-destroy, had been scheduled for eight that night, and our target was this happy-go-lucky ordinary little boy who sure didn't seem as though he needed to be rescued.

There wasn't anything I could do, either, to delay our attack, or change it. Felix would ask me whether or not what I'd seen was true. I would have to say yes. Then he would ask me whether there was any reason not to go through with everything. I would have to say no.

Maybe the difference between us was that Felix looked on everything as an exciting adventure that he could control and brag about afterward.

But it was I who wanted Batista to be safe. There really wasn't anything I could blame Felix for. After all, he was only acting as a friend, helping me out. What *I* had seen was what was pushing us all.

The telephone in Ms. Denton's office rang. I watched her half-run in to answer it. Within seconds, she was back out, pulling a raincoat over her shoulders, her forehead creased darkly. She spun suddenly and ran back for her purse and then disappeared out the front door. Strange.

The day was overcast and cool. I spent a little time playing with Stephanie. She really had been abused, enough so that her behavior toward men changed, was noticeable, was worried over. And yet there we were, a boy and a little girl, reading and counting and playing with each other. Whatever had happened to her was something she was handling, or at least seemed to be on the outside. Why wouldn't that be true of Batista, too?

When you think of it, how many kids, say, get spanked or shouted at or grounded and manage somehow to grow up O.K.? They don't carry around a lot of scars or resentment. They grow up with their families, with their parents, and seem to get along.

If you want to know, I was getting cold feet.

At naptime I stretched alongside Esteban with another counting book. As sweet as ever, he lay on his back, his hands crossed one atop the other on his chest, as I held out the numbers on the pages so he could see. I pointed. "*Cuatro*," I said.

He raised his right hand and a tiny little finger approached the picture of four spotted ponies. "Four," he said in his musical, high little voice.

"Four?"

"Four."

I looked down at him. He was smiling proudly. I flipped back in the book. I held up its first page and pointed.

"One," said Esteban.

I was so pleased I couldn't believe it. How did he get this far this fast in only four days? Who else had been working with him? I turned the page.

"Two," he told me.

Incredible! Maybe just by being at Sidewalk's End all kinds of things had floated into his mind.

"Three," he went on after a minute.

I couldn't remember when I had learned to count or to read. Probably Esteban wouldn't remember, either. But I would remember when *he* had. How he learned might be a mystery, but where wasn't.

"Seven," said Esteban in his now drowsy singsong. The

picture before him was of six cats sitting in sunshine and licking their paws.

Well, maybe I had expected too much too soon. Then again, from one to four was a great start. I started to say something to him when I noticed his eyes had closed and his breathing had grown deep.

Tomorrow.

I crept away from Esteban's mattress and tiptoed back down into the play area. I must have been smiling to myself because Debbie waved me over to her side. "What's up?" she asked.

"Esteban has learned some numbers. In English."

"Good for him." She brought up a knee and locked her fingers around it.

"Can I ask you something?"

"Sure, Ben, what?"

"Well, I don't mean to criticize, but the food the kids get isn't very—well, I know about the four food groups and all, but it sure doesn't seem very healthy or…nourishing. I mean, there's so much cheese and butter on everything, and cholesterol is so—"

Debbie nodded and raised a hand to stop me. "Remember," she said nicely, "most of what we have here is being donated. We don't have money enough to buy vegetables or meats or a lot of fresh fruit. Actually, sometimes the stuff we get is awful. I've pulled maggots out of oranges, scraped blue mold off bread, thrown away tin cans that I was afraid to open. But the people who send the stuff to us take its value off their income taxes just the same. We're sort of like a toxic dump," she said, laughing.

"That's not funny. It's too much starch and—"

Debbie nodded quickly. "I know, I know. But we do our best, Ben, really. And we always have hope."

A tiny shriek followed by a scattering of little forms told us two things: naptime was over and Buster was on the loose!

Neither of us saw who had opened his cage. But judging from the patterns of kids crisscrossing the room, it was likely to have been Max, who stood near the emptied wire-mesh rectangle watching his troops decide whether to run from or to chase the shadowy furry creature skittering around the edges of the room. There was a thin, quirky smile on Max's lips, grown-up almost, as though he had designed this test to see who had guts and who hadn't.

Miguel and Esteban had. Together, carefully and on tiptoes, they stalked Buster along one wall and toward a corner. They got down on their hands and knees as they closed in. Buster stood on his hind legs, his whiskers aquiver, his paws held up in front of him as though he were a prizefighter tensed to bob and weave and then throw a punch. But before he could, Esteban launched himself.

Buster didn't take even a second to consider. He wasn't a rat for nothing. He turned tail as though he had heard gunfire, and in his panic he ran right into the waiting hands of Miguel who laughed as his fingers closed around the squirming little rodent.

I took a step forward, thinking that Buster would take a mean bite out of Miguel's hand. I needn't have worried. Miguel was a natural animal handler, letting his fingers part enough so that Buster could stick his head up and out of his temporary prison to look around. Seeing daylight must have calmed his nerves. Miguel marched proudly toward the table on which sat Buster's cage and, as Esteban held open the mesh door to its limit, deposited Buster very gently back into his forest of newspaper and lettuce leaves.

"We won't have to teach those two the concept of teamwork, will we?" Debbie asked, smiling proudly.

I shook my head and smiled back. And yet I was conscious of a sudden sympathy for Buster.

There he was, each and every day, caged, not in control of his natural life. He was tame and gentle, I suppose, for a rat. But each day, when the kids arrived, his nerves must tighten, his muscles tense. Maybe today, maybe finally, someone would be a little more clumsy, a little slower. When he was fed, when fingers opened his door and slipped in his daily ration of greens, there just might be that extra second. He could jump, make a break, run for it. He might exist on lettuce, but he probably lived on hope.

Hope was what was sinking in my heart as the day ended. I could see myself at Irene's house, eating a foreign taste-treat, and then leaving with Felix for an after-dinner ride. I could imagine us wheeling around the neighborhood, looking at our wristwatches, waiting for the right moment to turn south. I could picture us hanging about in the shadows outside the Mission Felicidad, waiting until eight o'clock precisely and then slipping through the gap in the fence. I could even visualize Teddy waving at us from the back porch of the mission, bringing us in secretly.

But I never got to see the end of that movie. I was standing all alone not far from Buster's cage. "How's the day gone?"

I nearly leapt out of my skin. I turned to see Ms. Denton dragging her arm out of the sleeve of her raincoat and standing just outside her office.

"Fine."

"Good." Without looking, she threw her coat backward into her office. "Do you think you could stay a few minutes later tonight, Ben? There's something I need to talk about."

Before I could give her an answer, she was walking toward

me and then past, quickly patting my shoulder as she went toward the door that led to the play-yard.

After an hour or so of out-of-doors playtime, parents began to arrive. Once again, despite every good intent, I missed seeing who picked up Batista. Well, never mind, I told myself. I'd know soon enough.

I wasn't the only person who had been asked to stay late. When all the kids had gone home, Ms. Denton stood in the center of the round multicolored play-rug waiting as we assembled: Mrs. Mendoza, Frank, Debbie, and I.

"Let's sit down, shall we?" Ms. Denton suggested, her long narrow frame folding onto the rug so quickly you would have thought she had fainted.

The rest of us followed her lead, a little slower and probably a lot less gracefully, too. I was sitting between Frank and Debbie. Mrs. Mendoza sat on the other side of Frank.

We waited. We all looked at Ms. Denton, who looked back at us silently. Suddenly she broke off eye contact and looked down at her hands. She examined her fingertips. We could all see they were trembling. The only time I'd seen this before was when someone was sick or angry, so angry he or she couldn't speak. Ms. Denton didn't look angry.

She shrugged. She looked up at the four of us. "We lost a client today," she said very quietly.

No one spoke. Finally Frank did. "Who?"

"Wendell," Ms. Denton answered.

"Where did he go?" I asked.

Ms. Denton smiled and then her eyes filled with tears. "I suppose it depends on what you believe, Ben," she said.

A sick familiar feeling came from somewhere, from years past.

"What happened?" Debbie asked in a whisper.

Ms. Denton shrugged again. "It's hard to say. The police aren't very clear about it."

"What about his family?" Mrs. Mendoza wanted to know.

"Only Wendell," Ms. Denton said.

"For God's sake, how?" This from Frank.

Ms. Denton seemed to be having a hard time organizing her thoughts. "Well," she began, "apparently it was in a fight of some kind. Well, not that, maybe, that sounds silly, doesn't it, a three-year-old in a fight to the death? But someone was angry enough, or maybe high or drunk enough, to do it."

If I was any judge, the four of us wanted to scream at her: Do what? We didn't need to.

"He was very badly beaten. And then"–she had to swallow hard and take an enormous gulp of air–"and then he was thrown out a window."

Jesus!

I don't think, I don't remember any of us looking at each other. We sat absolutely still in silence. There were no tears but for the few that ran down Ms. Denton's cheeks. The rest of us were in shock.

"I've spent most of the day with Wendell's family. And the police. Doug called me here just after we opened…just after…after Wendell was…reported."

Ms. Denton drew a handful of tissue from the pocket of her dress and blew her nose noisily. She sat up a little straighter. "Of course, the ironic thing is that we weren't focusing on Wendell at all. Benjamin's been worried about Batista. And we knew about Stephanie, didn't we? Oh, we all had our antennae up and active." She gave a sad, short little laugh. "Pointed in the wrong directions, it seems."

"There wasn't a way in the world we could have known,"

Frank said then firmly. "You can't anticipate these things. They just happen."

"I know, I know," Ms. Denton agreed, looking again at her hands. "But I feel so guilty! So useless!" She looked up quickly at Frank. "I'm supposed to be comforting you," she said with a trembly grin.

"We take comfort where we can find it," Frank replied.

"But I thought you couldn't drink or smoke or do drugs or anything in a shelter." Even as I heard myself speak, I realized how childish I sounded.

"What could we have done?" asked Mrs. Mendoza of us all. "We're not equipped to board children. We can't take them away from their families without cause." She stopped. "It wasn't someone in Wendell's own family, was it? The person who…did it?"

Ms. Denton shook her head, but then said, "We don't know for sure yet."

Debbie stretched out her hands and took one of Ms. Denton's. "I know this sounds hard, Lou," Debbie said softly, "but really, since we can't see these things coming, it's almost like a random accident, isn't it? I mean, we all joke about how easy it is to be hit by a bus. Well, Wendell got hit. I mean, that does sound harsh, but it's true. We can't let our own work, our own focus waver."

"You're right, I know," Ms. Denton agreed. "But it's so hard…."

Four heads nodded in unison. Ms. Denton withdrew her hand from Debbie's. "I just felt," she said next, "that you should all know at the same time, that I should be the one to tell you personally. We all have our own memories of Wendell. We all had our own relationships with him."

"Life," Frank said next. "That's all this is. Life. It's mean as hell. It's confusing and sad and exciting and miserable and satisfying and endlessly mysterious."

Ms. Denton stood up and then took a step forward to embrace Mrs. Mendoza, who hugged her back. A whole dance of changing partners and hugging began. I tried to hold back, but I was swept into the circle, anyway. I hugged everybody back, but just a little.

I can't be too clear about my feelings just at that moment. I felt rotten, of course, about what had happened. Worse, because I hadn't really been all that crazy about Wendell before. But now, mixed in with my guilt, was a stronger feeling. If I didn't get out of there in ten seconds I was going to explode.

I may have had reasons for worrying about Batista before, reasons colored a bit by Charley's long-ago disappearance. But now, nothing and no one was going to stand in my way.

chapter eighteen

I sat at Irene's table, spinning my wheels. I hadn't been able to tell Felix about Wendell yet. I hadn't been able to tell him that what we were planning wasn't an adventure, it was a rescue, real and serious.

Felix's mom served Swedish–ligonberries and meatballs and steamed noodles of some kind in a white sauce. Felix announced we were going outside to ride for a while. At seven-thirty we turned south toward downtown. By 7:32 I had relayed to Felix what had happened to Wendell. He hadn't needed anything cleared up. He got the message.

By five to eight we were in place, in the shadows under a tree across the street from the sideyard of the Mission Felicidad.

"This is your show, Benny," Felix whispered to me as we stood motionlessly, staring at the mission's back porch.

I didn't have to ask what he meant. His reasoning from the night before was still valid: only I knew what Batista looked like. Felix didn't; Teddy might have.

"Look!" Felix pointed. "There's Teddy! Go!"

I ran half-crouched across the street toward the wire fencing. A lock on a chain hung between the two gateposts, but there was enough room for me to slip through. Ahead I could see Teddy talking with a couple of older guys, using some kind of excuse to edge them back into the mission so we could follow them unnoticed.

I jumped up the few steps of the stoop toward Teddy. Then, praying under my breath but also eager to get the show on the road, I followed him inside. "O.K.!" Teddy whispered proudly. I tried to look past him at the war zone into which we were moving. Suddenly Teddy's hand was on my shoulder. I couldn't help myself: I jumped.

"Here's the deal," he whispered. "All you have to do is get in and sneak along the walls till you find your kid. Come back and tell me which he is and then we move."

I nodded. Teddy stood to one side; I took the first step.

I was in a kitchen, very large, bigger even than the one in my dad's restaurant. There were grown-ups sitting around a gigantic wooden trestle, having coffee and talking quietly. Their backs were to me so, on automatic, I pushed forward, taking a right.

Lights were dimmed. It was just eight o'clock but most people seemed ready to bed down for the night. I tiptoed along a wall, skirting the main central area.

I felt much safer than I had at the Navarre. There seemed to be order and purpose here. Even the air was different from the Navarre Hotel: clean, sweet-scented, a little baby talcum-powder smell mixing with the odors of bacon and onions, which I happen to like.

I edged carefully down a corridor along which were rooms every six feet or so. I passed one closed door before I realized that Batista could be behind it. How would I know?

My heart was thumping. I took a few steps back and knocked very gently on the door. Then, without waiting for any signal from within, I opened the door just a little. I peeked in.

A pretty woman, maybe ten years younger than Aunt Eileen, dressed in a robe and slippers, looked up from a lower bunk. She had a book open in her lap, and behind her I could make out the figures of two little six-year-olds. "Yes?" she asked pleasantly.

"Oh, nothing. Sorry." I said, backing out as fast as I could.

Other doors were half-open and as I tried slipping past like a shadow I peeked in: bunk beds, orange crates, clean clothes.

I reached the end of the corridor and had to turn one way or another. Ahead of me was the mission's front door, now locked. To its right was a big room with a television set playing softly. I stuck my head around the door frame to see maybe half a dozen people sitting quietly, watching something on a Spanish channel. No sign of Batista.

Silently I turned away and found myself standing at the end of the big room. Ahead of me were two rows of cribs. At the end of these were aisles and then more bunk beds. I figured parents slept in the bunks nearby to keep watch over their kids. There were clothing and towels hung from bed frames, shoes neatly tied together on the floor.

I was relieved. Batista would be in one of the cribs. All I had to do was find him and report back. Then Teddy and I would do whatever we were going to do and get out, fast.

I took a step forward, and then another.

In the fourth crib on the left lay Batista, sleeping peacefully, his mouth open. He wore pajama bottoms and a little T-shirt. His feet were kept warm by thin cotton socks.

I looked down at him for a long moment.

If my motor had been humming ever since hearing about Wendell, it revved to a roar now.

Without thinking more about it, I floored the pedal.

chapter nineteen

I reached into the crib and lifted Batista gently out, above the railing. I shifted his weight, trying to find a good balance for running. Then I ran like hell back toward the kitchen, Batista tucked under my right arm like a football.

I wasn't being sneaky or careful. In the back of my mind I pictured handing him off to Teddy somewhere along the line. Then I could sprint ahead, running interference, until we hit the open air and slipped through the gate. Felix would take over from there.

I hadn't many steps to run. I made it to the door of the kitchen. I saw Teddy waiting there, around the corner. I clutched Batista and, instead of handing him off, kept right on going, hanging a left and running toward the door to the stoop and the outside. I guess maybe I was determined to be a hero all by myself.

This may not have been a good idea.

I heard a woman's scream echoing through the kitchen behind me. "¡Batista! ¡Ayudame!"

Then somebody tackled me.

I had been almost ready to push through the door to the dark safety outside. Surprised, I instinctively rolled my body so that Batista wouldn't hit the floor first. All the lights in the mission went on at about the same second I hit the deck.

I wasn't hurt, just dazed and astonished. I held on to Batista for dear life as I heard a low, threatening mumble begin to swim toward me, footsteps and voices surrounding us.

I sat up slowly, interested in a strange, distant way to see who had brought me down so professionally, cradling a now awake but still sleepy Batista against my chest. In the growing confusion, I saw a head of brown curls and very clear skin. "You!"

Jennie Johnson backpedalled on her knees, taking shelter behind the forest of legs that was growing into the linoleum floor.

A tall man—from where I sat on the floor any man was tall—with glasses, no hair, wearing a cardigan sweater, materialized. He reached down and roughly started to pull me to my feet. Halfway up he changed his mind and grabbed at Batista instead. I pulled back. *He* pulled. Batista for the first time began to cry.

A woman who had to be Batista's mother came out of the crowd at a run and, ducking her shoulder like a linebacker, put it into my gut. I bounced off her, breathless, smashing into the door behind me. She reached out for Batista and caught him as he slipped from my arms. The room erupted with sound, half Spanish, wholly angry.

And then the lights went out.

I mean, they really did go out. The people in the mission at first said "Oooo!" all together and then the "oooo" changed and became "oww!" and then, "Wait a minute! What's the matter! Who put out the lights! Somebody put the lights on!"

Teddy grabbed me just as the lights were switched back on. "Come on!" he whispered urgently.

But by then the man with glasses had hold of my shoulder and one arm. I looked past him at a crowd of maybe twenty people, fat and thin, short and tall, fair and dark. Suddenly I knew what it felt like to be on the way to the nearest big tree to be lynched.

"Just what is going on here?" the man with glasses asked sternly.

Batista's mother said something in a scream and in Spanish so quickly that all I could register was "¡niño!"

Teddy Hines tried to separate me from the tall man but failed. The man held on tightly. Teddy looked across me at the angry face. "It's O.K., Mr. George. Really."

"What do you mean it's O.K., Teddy?" the man with glasses demanded hotly. "Was this kid trying to kidnap Batista? What is he doing here at all? Who let him in?"

Teddy bravely looked Mr. George straight in the eye. "I let him in," he said smoothly. "Batista was in danger."

A tremor of thunder ran along the edges of the crowd in the kitchen. "Danger? Who from? What's the kid say? We ought to call the cops!"

Uh-oh!

The image of Doug Bailey floated across my mind. Actually, at that moment I would have been glad to see him.

"He means well," said a timid voice from behind the mob.

"Mr. George," Teddy said very quietly, "this little boy was being abused. My friend here, Benjamin, witnessed it."

"Witnessed what?" asked Mr. George sternly.

Jennie pushed her way into the circle. "He saw him in a supermarket," she explained less timidly. "His mother had hit him and Batista fell into a stack of canned goods."

"Who are *you?*" Mr. George wanted to know.

"I'm one of Benjamin's friends. Teddy brought me."

Mr. George turned his bespectacled eyes from Jennie to me. Then he looked again at Teddy. Finally he let go of my arm and wiped the top of his shiny head. "Is that true?"

"What?" I asked.

"That you saw the little boy hit."

I nodded.

"When?" Mr. George asked.

The noises of anger and arousal around us had quieted. People were listening now. There wasn't any doubt I was still likely to be carted off to public execution, but at least I was getting a chance at a trial.

"Monday night. I saw him flying through the air. I heard him screaming as he landed."

Mr. George just stared. Finally he let go of my shoulder. I wanted to run, and I could feel Teddy's fingers tighten on my arm, but we couldn't have made a break. There were too many people standing around, some of them behind us, blocking our escape.

Mr. George took a few steps away from me. The people standing at alert, elbow to elbow, parted to let him walk out of the kitchen and back into the crib area, where Batista's mother was seated on a lower bunk near the crib from which I had snatched him, holding him against her body.

Teddy pushed me and we both followed Mr. George. I didn't hear Mr. George's first question to Batista's mother, but whatever it was, it caught her attention. She clasped Batista more tightly to her and looked angrily up at the mission's night supervisor. "*¡Nunca!*" she snapped hoarsely.

"You better get out of here!" Jennie whispered in my ear.

I didn't turn to look at her. "Thanks very much," I said out of the side of my mouth. "What are you doing here, anyway?"

"Teddy told me what was going on. I couldn't let you do this."

There was no time to argue about any of this because just then Mr. George turned around and reached back for my arm. "I think you better hear this," he told me severely. He pulled me toward the bunk beds.

"Now, slowly," Mr. George said to Batista's mother, "exactly what happened?"

"I can tell you what happened," I offered. "I saw him flying through the air. I heard him land. I heard him screaming!"

Batista's mother still held him like something very valuable made out of glass. She reached out so suddenly I didn't have time to leap backward. She had me in her grip and pulled me down, crash! onto my knees on the hardwood floor so that she could look me directly in the face. "*¿Estás loco?*" she demanded in a rough whisper. "Are you crazy?"

"I saw it," I defended.

Batista's mother pointed to the bed above her own. I looked up to see Batista's sisters, one of whom had been in the bodega only a few days before.

The crowd around us was silent, waiting.

I looked back at Batista's mother, puzzled. She nodded at me, very satisfied, very proud. Then she looked up at Mr. George. "*Diga, por favor,*" she directed. "You talk better."

"But, Carmela, I think you–," Mr. George started to say.

Batista's mother shrugged her shoulders and looked back at me. She spoke very slowly, choosing unfamiliar words.

"Batista's sister was…" She took one hand from around Batista and pushed at me, her fingers firm against my chest. "*¿Comprende?* Batista stands…holding on to…wire. The wire. Cage. So, Gabriella gives Batista big ride. Very fast. *Entonces,* for joke, she stops fast, very sudden. Batista goes backward. It was so strong. The stop."

I didn't believe what she said. It must have showed.

"*¡Sabes nada!*" Batista's mother told me. "*Batista es niño. Hombre.* He is…*esperanzo*…hope."

"But his sisters," Jennie started to say, standing behind me. "What about them?"

Carmela nodded. "Batista is man. It's for him. I have never hit Batista. *¡Nunca!* I will never do it."

"And his sisters?" Jennie asked. She was persistent.

"They know better," Batista's mother said shortly.

"So, Benjamin, do you see now?" Mr. George asked somberly. "What you saw really was an accident, a joke that went a little wrong."

Batista's mother grabbed my hand and squeezed it hard. "Leave us," she said firmly. "No trouble. From nobody. Leave us!"

chapter twenty

Batista's mother let go of my hand. I stood up. There was silence in the room.

"Let me through!"

Heads turned quickly. Mine, too.

I saw the uniform first. Oh no! Someone had called the cops. I looked up, ready to see Doug Bailey's face.

But the man I saw was white and thin; his uniform was badly cut and too big for him. He was all Adam's apple and raw bone. Still, he was a cop. And behind him stood Felix, looking around rather timidly.

"So, Alan," said the policeman to Mr. George but definitely looking my way, "what's this all about?"

I looked down at the tops of my shoes.

"I think we've handled it, Sergeant," Mr. George said then. "It seems to have been a case of well-intentioned error."

When I looked up, the policeman was still examining me. "You're sure?" he asked.

Mr. George nodded.

"All right, Alan, if you say so. Come on, kid, we'd better have a little talk."

He took my arm. Together we edged our way through the crowd, passing through the mission's kitchen again and finally out onto the back stoop. Felix was trailing us, as were Teddy and Jennie.

The screen door closed. Lights from inside the mission shone out on us in a triangle. Other lights—which really startled me—whirled at us from the top of the police car which was parked just outside the gate. The policeman let my arm go. Mr. George himself stood in the doorway to listen. I looked quickly at Felix, feeling I should apologize or something. But the look on his face made me turn around.

There was Doug Bailey!

It's amazing how fast one can go from panic to relief to panic again.

"Well, I'll be damned!" Doug Bailey said. A smile flickered on his lips. "What are you doing here, Ben?"

"It's a long story."

Doug Bailey put his huge hand on my shoulder, guiding me down the steps away from the mission. He looked back over his shoulder. "You kids better wait a minute. I may need to speak with you."

We walked a few more steps into the darkness. Then we stopped. "O.K., son, just what was all this about?"

It took a moment. "It was about trying to save a little boy from being badly treated. *Another* little boy," I added, sort of hitting his memory over the head. Doug Bailey frowned. Then he nodded. "All right. And?"

I took me maybe two minutes to give Officer Bailey the story of Batista. I didn't have to mention Wendell again.

"So, what were you going to do? You rescue Batista and then what?"

I shrugged. I felt sort of stupid, but I was also angry. "Whatever it was would have been better than what happened last night!"

Doug Bailey shook his head as though he were puzzled. "You know, Ben, everything you say makes sense, up to that very point. Suppose for a minute you were right about what you thought had happened to Batista. And then suppose you had, as the saying goes, taken the law into the your own hands. How do you think that would appear?"

Wait a minute! I thought. I'm the good guy here! Still, I knew what he was getting at. "Not very good," I allowed.

"You could have been in big trouble."

"Batista could have been in bigger trouble."

Doug Bailey grinned. "When the do-good bug hits, it never loosens its grip."

"What's that supposed to mean? You do good."

"True, but I'm an adult, Ben. I've been trained. Gone to school. I've had more time and experience than you."

"I don't feel sorry," I said. "If I had been right, someone would have had to do something, and no one was. It would have been up to me."

"Or someone a lot like you."

I looked down at the tops of my sneakers.

"Did you tell anyone you met Batista at Sidewalk's End?" Doug Bailey asked after a few seconds.

I tried to remember. "I don't think so."

"Good."

I looked back to see Felix, Jennie, and Teddy in a sort of huddle. The mist was moving in from the ocean and the temperature was dropping. One of the amazing things about living in California, along the coast, is that when the sun goes down it gets really chill. Then, maybe an hour later, the air warms and the nights can be scented even in December with wildflowers.

"I think that's probably the best thing you can do, too, Ben," Doug Bailey was saying.

I was kind of startled, my mind elsewhere. "What?"

"Go back to Sidewalk's End first thing in the morning. Well, maybe not exactly at seven-thirty. I don't think I'd like Batista's mother to see you first thing when she drops him off."

"What happens...what are you going to do...er, say?"

"To whom?"

"Do you have to make a report? Am I going to have a record?"

Officer Bailey laughed softly. "No, I don't imagine you will. If you're asking whether I'll call Lou Denton, well, maybe. After all, this concerns one of her charges."

"But nothing happened!" I pleaded.

"Hey, Ben, it's all right. She'll understand, I know. Look, what you did was not very well thought out, I admit, but it came from your heart. And no harm was done. You don't have to be ashamed of anything."

I wasn't ashamed, but suddenly I thought about my grandmother. Of all the people in the world, she was the one I didn't want to know about this. "Do you kids need a ride home?" Doug Bailey asked next.

I looked up at him. "Not me. I've got my bike. Maybe you could drive Jennie to her house. That would be nice."

"What about your other friend?"

"Felix has a bike."

"The blond kid."

"Teddy?" I was stumped. "I don't know," I said haltingly. I didn't want to give anything away. "Maybe you should ask him."

Officer Bailey turned us both back around toward the mission.

It didn't take very long to make arrangements. Jennie had come with Teddy—no bicycles. Officer Bailey and his pal would drive her home. Teddy said that he only lived a few blocks away. Doug Bailey had no reason to question him further. Felix began to slide off the back stoop like wax from a candle, edging toward the gate through which we had slipped.

"Thanks for your help," I whispered at Jennie as she came down the steps.

She stopped and looked angrily at me. "I did it for you, Ben. Don't you get it? You could have been in a lot of trouble."

"You didn't *know* that."

"Yes, I did."

"How?" I demanded.

Jennie put both of her hands on her hips and leaned toward me, whispering very quickly. "Because I snuck in with Teddy and looked around before I hid. There isn't one child in this mission who isn't adored by his family."

"You couldn't know that."

"But I did. Call it intuition."

"Coming, miss?" Bailey's partner called out.

I stood a moment more looking at Jennie, who stared back at me. Finally, I grinned. "You throw a mean tackle."

She nodded. "I know. I don't get to do that anymore as often as I like."

"I'm grateful."

There was a tiny moment between us. "See you," Jennie said finally, very softly. I nodded. She turned and started across the paved yard toward the gate and the police car with its red and blue lights still swirling on its roof.

I glanced at Felix who was standing in the shadows across

the street, poised to jump on his bike. I waved at him, telling him to go ahead. Then I turned back to Teddy. "Why'd you have to tell Jennie what we were doing?"

"I thought she might help us, be a diversion," Teddy answered smoothly.

"Where are you going now?"

Teddy shrugged. "Home."

"Where's that?"

"Not far."

"Where?" I insisted.

"Who cares?" Teddy dodged.

I decided not to press. Later I would. "Did you have dinner?" I asked then.

Teddy shook his head. "I forgot. With all the planning and watching the clock and all."

"Come on," I said. "Get on my bike. We'll go see my dad."

chapter twenty-one

"This is really good," Teddy said, lifting a spicy chicken wing toward his mouth.

We were seated at an indoor table in a corner, out of the way. Dad had been surprised to see me so late, but he hadn't asked too many questions in front of Teddy. Besides, the restaurant was crowded, so he didn't have a lot of attention to give either of us.

"Go on," I said, watching Teddy's lips pucker from the hot sauce. He reached for his glass of water. "Then what happened?"

Teddy swallowed some liquid and wiped his fingers on his big paper napkin. "Nothing."

"What do you mean, nothing? Your dad lost his job. That's not nothing."

Teddy blinked. He looked up and around Dad's restaurant. "I don't want to talk about it," he said quietly, slowly.

"Why not? What could be so terrible?"

Teddy stared at me. I stared him down. "Well, if you have to know, after that nothing happened. Dad looked and looked for another job in Santa Maria but he couldn't find one. He had good skills but no one was hiring. Instead, guys were being laid off all over."

"But he had a family to care for," I said stupidly. "Didn't people understand that?"

"Sure," Teddy agreed. "But money's the bottom line, Ben. If things are tough and your company's losing dough, you can't let feelings make your decisions. Even Dad understood that."

"And you were only nine?"

"Just about turning ten," Teddy decided after a moment.

"So how did you all get down here?"

"Well," Teddy replied, "we stayed up north for more than a year, almost two. Dad looked. My mom went out to get a job and didn't have much better luck. But my sister and I were in school and they thought it was best to stay where we were and keep trying."

"But what about unemployment and part-time work? What about employment agencies? Didn't anyone help?"

Teddy closed his eyes and sat back. "They tried, I guess." His plate was still full of chicken and tostadas and peppers.

"So?" I prompted. "So, what happened?"

"You sure you want to hear all this?"

"Yes, I am. We're friends, aren't we?"

Teddy's eyebrow did a little one-sided jump as though he wasn't exactly sure this was true. Then I guess he made up his mind. He leaned forward and put both elbows on the table. "Well, after a while it began to get to my dad."

"I see."

"No, you don't, Ben," Teddy warned. "Not really. It got him down, made him sad, made him doubt he could take care of us ever again."

"But things change!"

"Yeah, but sometimes not fast enough. We were out of money, out of savings. Not that we had a lot of loot piled up, you understand. But we still had our house. Then, one day, we didn't."

"I don't get it."

Teddy shrugged. "Dad told me we couldn't keep making mortgage payments. We didn't have money coming in. We had to tell the bank. They'd been patient, I guess, waiting maybe four or five months. But finally they took back the house."

"Where did you go?"

"To my dad's folks," Teddy said. "But that wasn't good. It made Dad feel worse. I mean, they have a small house and suddenly you pile in four more bodies and people get sort of edgy, you know? Short-tempered. Everything becomes a big deal. It was more than Dad could stand."

"But it was only temporary."

"Temporary after a while begins to look permanent." Teddy paused and leaned back. "So the three of us came down to Santa Barbara."

"Three?"

"My dad didn't make the trip."

"Why not?"

Teddy closed his eyes and sat absolutely still for the longest time. "Why not?" I asked again. "Why didn't he come with you?"

Teddy inhaled a big breath and let it out in a long sigh. Then he opened his eyes and looked directly into mine. "Because one night he went out in his truck. He drove into the hills above town. He shot himself."

At first I couldn't think of anything to say. Everything I thought of sounded, in my mind, not good enough, stupid. "Oh, no."

Teddy nodded.

"But if he'd waited, if he'd had hope…"

"He had used it all up."

"But…but what about all of you? How could he desert you like that?"

Teddy closed his eyes again, I think to hide tears. "I don't know. I've thought about that. I expect he thought he was making life simpler."

We sat silently a moment. Then Teddy opened his eyes and focused on his plate again. He leaned forward and picked up a chicken wing and took a small bite from it. "I never saw him," he said quietly. "They wouldn't let us. Mom did. But not Elaine or me."

I still couldn't think of a thing to say that would make any of this easier.

"So," Teddy sighed again, "that's how we got here. Mom cleaned up the truck and packed us into it and headed south. She's studying to be a nurse when she isn't working. Elaine and I are in school. We live in the truck. We move it every day but mostly we keep it near the water. The sound of the ocean makes Mom feel good."

Teddy cut into one of his peppers and ate a moment. He wiped his mouth and leaned back again. "That's why I needed to work at the hospice," he said next.

"What? Why? I don't get it."

At first Teddy smiled. I was slow in seeing his eyes begin to fill again. "I never said good-bye to him, you see. My dad. I never saw him–dead."

"But–"

"I needed to know, Ben," Teddy continued, cutting me off. "I needed to see and to feel and…I know this sounds creepy, but I needed to say good-bye to Dad through other people. Kind of send messages with them, you see?"

Teddy steadied himself. "It didn't hit me right away. But I thought about it in class that day, and it all made sense. I could learn from others, I could help them, make them happy the way I couldn't my dad. It's a little selfish, maybe, not to mention weird, I know. But I need it."

I heard all this but I was back about twenty paces. "Wait a minute! Why should you have to stay in your truck when there are places like Mission Felicidad?"

Teddy reached out with his fingers to the last chunk of pepper. "We've stayed there," he said before finishing it. "We've stayed about everywhere you can. But you can't stay places forever. There are limits. Other people need a break, too, from time to time. Believe it or not, some people are worse off than we are. At least we're healthy, all of us. We're in school. My mom works when she can. The truck is paid for."

"Geez!" I had a sudden thought. "It's nearly ten! She's probably going crazy wondering where you are right now!"

Teddy smiled. "She's cool. She and Elaine went to a movie. She won't worry for a while yet."

"We should call her."

Teddy laughed. "Ben, we don't have a phone in the truck."

To say I felt dumb is too easy.

But then one of those miracle light bulbs went on in my mind. I finished my drink and thought at the same time.

There wasn't a reason in the world why it couldn't be done.

Teddy rode home on my bike.

That was my suggestion. My dad's was that he would be happy to get up early the next day to drive me down to Sidewalk's End.

Dad let me hang around the restaurant for a while and then, early for him, he decided he would leave to go home, too.

"You haven't told me about your day," he said offhandedly as we drove.

I sat beside him in silence. The first thing I thought of was to mention Charley. That suddenly a minute had come—the minute I was standing near Batista's crib—when the Family Curse, the Derby Squint, made sense. In that one second I knew why people looked at me that way, what they expected me to finally understand. I could tell him about Wendell then, too, and lastly about Batista.

"Well?" Dad prompted.

But the weight, the embarrassment of what had happened at Mission Felicidad hit me. I fought against self-pity and regret. Even though I had been wrong, I was wrong for good reasons. I wouldn't ever back down on that. Aunt Eileen often calls me "stubbun." I guess I am. "It was busy," I said after a second.

"Are you still enjoying it?"

"Yeah, in a strange way."

"Why strange?"

"Odd things. Like this afternoon, finding out one of the little Latino boys had learned to count in English. He must have picked things out of the air, but he did. That made me feel good."

"Helping people does, you know," Dad said, turning into our driveway.

I grabbed at the ring.

"Hey, Dad, what would you do if you knew someone, someone personally, who was homeless?"

"What do you mean?" he asked, getting out of the car and letting its door slam.

"Just what I said," I replied, following him. We started up the front steps. "If someone you knew really well was having a hard time, not because of anything he'd done, what would you do?"

"Try to help him, Ben."

I smiled. I knew he would say that.

chapter twenty-two

I didn't push him.

Every kid learns when and how far and how fast to try to get a parent to do what he wants. I 'planted the seed' and said good night.

Of course, it wasn't easy sleeping. Partly I was anxious, hoping Dad would understand how simple and easy it would be to do what I had thought of. And how good for others.

Then, too, I had held back on the ride home. I guess maybe I was afraid Dad would think I'd gone overboard. That being at Sidewalk's End wasn't "good" for me. That I was coming up with wild ideas, acting like a tornado, blowing hard and fast and who cared where its path crashed or what damage was done.

If he even began to think that way, he would reject my idea.

Ordinarily when something that seems reasonable to me doesn't to Dad, I shrug and come around from another direction until I've been turned down three or four times. Then I wait a couple of days before trying the whole process all over again. If I still get nowhere, sooner or later I have to shrug it off and tell myself, Well, O.K., later, another idea, another time. I guess that this means I accept that Dad sees something in an idea I don't, that he's protecting me in a way. I can accept that.

But I didn't want to now, with this idea.

The other reason I had trouble sleeping that Thursday night was that I still had to get through Friday, my last day at Sidewalk's End.

I was certain Doug Bailey would call Ms. Denton and tell her what had gone down at the mission. I could almost imagine how she would take the news. She wouldn't be happy. But she knew how I felt, what I was convinced had been happening. How dangerous that was. That it had to be stopped. O.K., maybe I had acted a little wild. Still and all. . .

Then I thought about Felix. The kidnapping had been his idea, not mine. I'd known something had to be done for Batista, but I hadn't reached the same conclusion Felix had. That was Felix: fast, sure, more "stubbun" even than I was.

I gave a couple of minutes to trying to blame everything that had happened on Felix but not with a lot of success. Especially not after what had happened to Wendell.

Then I remembered how Jennie had knocked me breathless when she'd tackled me. I smiled.

And that was how I went to sleep.

I didn't move when the alarm went off. I reached up and hit the snooze button, but of course I couldn't snooze. I had to get up and, according to Doug Bailey, slowly make my way down to Sidewalk's End. I was not to arrive before Batista and his mother, and most especially not before Batista's mother had left the center.

Nigel was lying on the end of my bed, stretched out flat on

his back, his forepaws curled neatly on his chest, his legs spread wide apart. This was irresistible. I reached down to poke his white furry underbelly.

All four paws shot up into the air. I pulled back with Nigel's claws snagged on my pajama sleeve. His bushy ringed-tail was thrashing in the air. He was mad.

I jumped out of bed but Nigel jumped down, too, on the attack. Before I could run out of my room to the john, he had launched himself straight at my ankles. He bit. "Nigel!"

I laughed and dodged and tried to push him away to make my way to safety but he followed, throwing himself again and again at my legs.

The day had begun.

True to his word the night before, Dad was up, dressed, and had coffee in his travelling mug before I came into the kitchen. "Well," he said, opening the refrigerator and pulling out a pitcher of orange juice, "this is your last day of vacation."

"Don't remind me."

"I think it's been a worthwhile project, don't you?"

"I guess."

"You sounded more positive last night."

"I'm still asleep."

"Have some toast with that. Want eggs or bacon?"

"No, thanks."

"We have time."

I wasn't all that hungry but I pretended. Dad went to work happily, pulling out a frying pan, having decided I should have both eggs and bacon...in this case, what he called "dirty eggs." These are not for dieters. You cook bacon first and then pull the strips out and put them in a warm oven; leaving the grease in the frying pan, you break a couple of eggs into the fat and cover them. You sort of roll the fat around and over the eggs and by the time your toast is up and ready to be buttered, you've got eggs-over-easy without having to take the chance of actually flipping them and breaking their yolks.

I'm sure Dad knows this whole meal is a killer. I also know he loves making it. I figured I wouldn't miss more than a couple of weeks off the end of my life.

As Dad cooked and I set out a little silverware, we listened to the morning news. Then, both our plates wearing little snips of parsley and orange wedges–Dad's idea of the difference between eating and dining–we sat down.

"How is it?"

He already knew, but it was easy, and true, to answer anyway. "Terrific," I said, breaking a corner of toast off to soak up a little egg yolk. As I put away a few more bites, remembering again I wasn't supposed to arrive too soon at Sidewalk's End, the radio announcer began to read something about a three-year-old child having been the victim of fatal child abuse the day before.

I leaned forward in my chair quickly, speaking a little louder than normal. "Dad, remember what I asked you last night?"

"What?"

"About what you'd do if someone you knew was suddenly homeless."

"Oh, sure. What about it?"

"Well, someone I know is homeless."

"Really? Who?"

"That kid who came to the restaurant last night, Teddy Hines."

Dad's eyebrows were raised just a bit.

"Worse, Dad," I rushed on. "When his dad lost his job, he killed himself!"

"No! That poor kid!"

I nodded. "We have to do something to help him."

"Is he all alone in the world?"

"No, he's got a mother and a little sister. They live in a truck down at the beach."

Dad sipped his coffee slowly and then stood up and walked to the stove, where he topped off his mug. "I'm only guessing, of course, but my hunch is that you've got an idea. Go ahead. Hit me."

"Well." I was sort of slow to start. I wanted to hold back a little, have a Plan B. "I thought the least we could do is bring them up and let them park their truck behind the restaurant. Teddy says his mother likes being near the ocean but I can't believe it's all that safe down there. Besides, they could have something to eat every day that way, too. They wouldn't have to worry about it or pay for it."

Dad's eyes widened but whatever he was about to say he swallowed. After a second of thought, he smiled. "Let me think about it, Ben. I'm not saying no. But I doubt whether the city would allow us to let someone actually live in the parking lot."

"Well, maybe when you close, they could come inside."

Dad laughed gently and took a few steps to put his hand on my shoulder. "Let's think about all this, kiddo. Maybe between the two of us we can come up with something a little better, something that's less like charity and more like real help."

"You mean a job?"

"Hey, slow down, Ben. Let me think a bit, O.K.?"

"Sure, I guess."

Dad laughed more loudly then, shaking his head. I must have surprised him. He suddenly remembered Eileen was still sleeping, and covered his mouth. I figured now was the time to hit him with Plan B. Let him choose. "Or we could do something else."

"Such as?"

"Well, they could bring the truck up here!"

Dad leaned against a counter and sipped his coffee, waiting. I smiled as widely as I dared, not wanting to go overboard. "You know what else we could do?"

Dad grinned. "I shudder to think."

I ignored that. "We could give Teddy's mother a job here, pay her a little something every week to take care of the house. That way Aunt Eileen wouldn't have to work so hard. She'd have more free time. She'd be happier."

Dad sighed. "Then we might as well bring them into the guest room. No sense in sending them out to a cold truck night after night when they've gotten so comfortable inside, is there?"

I could tell Dad was teasing. It didn't make me happy.

"Don't look so downhearted, Ben. I haven't said no to either idea."

"Well. . ."

"Look, kiddo, what you want to do comes from the right place. I told you I'm always on your side, on your team. Let's think about all this. Let's talk to Eileen, too. That would be only fair, don't you think? Ben?"

"I suppose so."

"I promise we'll come up with something that will help your friend. But we want to be careful at the same time. We don't want him and his family to be uncomfortable about anything, whatever we decide. After all, they have their own lives and their own choices to make."

"But Teddy's mother could go to school. She's studying nursing. If she didn't have to worry every day—"

"Ben, I told you. Rest easy. Let's give your ideas a chance to ripen. You're talking about three people in Teddy's family, and the three of us here. That's six people who need to be considered. All I'm saying is that we should be sure of what we're doing, sure that what we offer is the best for everyone concerned. That's not too bad a start, is it?"

"No, I guess not."

"Well, then, we'd better hit the trail. We're already late as it is. Those little kids will probably worry themselves sick if you don't show up soon."

I doubted it.

chapter twenty-three

I stood looking at the outside of Sidewalk's End. Nothing new, nothing different. No one looking out the window, waiting for me to show up. No ghost hovering.

There was nothing to do but take that first step. I opened the door and shucked off my windbreaker. Debbie and Frank saw me come in and both smiled their greetings. The kids were seated around the table having breakfast, Debbie in between Batista and Miguel, Frank being sandwiched by LaKesha and Barbara. Freida was in the kitchen.

I slid in between Esteban and Max. "Sleepyhead," Max teased in his croaking voice. "My dad would whip your ass."

I smiled. I looked around, wondering where Ms. Denton was. Missing. *That* made me a little nervous.

Esteban's orange juice was running down his chin and onto his sweatshirt. I grabbed a napkin and wiped his face.

I considered: either Ms. Denton was in conference somewhere with Doug Bailey, or reporting me to Mr. Walston, the man who had talked her into having me in the first place. I couldn't imagine anything else.

Breakfast was finished in fairly short order, and Debbie folded herself up on the rug in the big center space to read us our story. After a while I felt as I had on my very first day–like just another kid listening, eager, anxious, happy.

By nine-thirty, Ms. Denton still had not arrived and yet no one seemed to notice. I was cracking inside. Surely Debbie and Frank knew about last night. "Where's Ms. Denton?" I asked finally.

Frank shrugged, unworried.

"There's a board meeting," Debbie explained.

Oh, swell. It wasn't enough to have to explain to the board how Wendell could have slipped through our fingers. Now they would hear that one of their volunteers had gone off the deep end.

The whole morning seemed to go by like a new bottle of ketchup, forcing you to pound and slap and swear before you can get it flowing. Mrs. Mendoza arrived a little before eleven. And shortly after that, Debbie announced a walk to the park.

We all lined up to put on our sweaters or jackets. Debbie picked up a picnic basket from Freida, full of juices in cartons and cookies, while Frank collected a couple of rubber balls. Mrs. Mendoza and I zipped kids up, snapped them in, and paired them off, hand in hand. In ten minutes our little band was strung out on the sidewalk, headed toward the park where we had spent my very first morning. Everything we did made me remember my first day, which made me think of the struggle between Wendell and me as we had walked back from the beach. I remembered, too, turning his key. "Hey, dude!" If the police hit a dead end, maybe this would be a clue to help them.

We played in a warm spring mist that eventually cleared. Batista entertained himself as he had before, completely happy all alone chasing a soccer ball, skying it with his head, kneeing it, dribbling across the grass. Every so often Miguel or Max would chase him and try to steal the ball from him, but Batista's feet were just too quick for that and he would bounce giggling on his way, the ball still in his possession.

Debbie read a story in the bandshell. Frank followed Batista around to make certain the ball didn't fly out into the street or over a fence onto the baseball field. I kept my eyes glued to Max when he climbed his tree and began giving orders to Miguel and Esteban.

All in all, it was a sort of usual morning. Only my stomach reminded me that, as Aunt Eileen would have said, another shoe was going to drop. Sometime.

When the kids were asleep, or at least resting with their eyes closed, and while Debbie, Frank, and Mrs. Mendoza still lay or sat dreamily next to their charges, listening to classical music, I tiptoed out into the large story room. Buster snuffled in his cage.

I had had a wonderful thought. Well, not wonderful, because it sounds mean-spirited, but good enough. Ms. Denton had a cold, or the flu. After all, if a child couldn't stay at the center when he or she was ill, for fear of infecting others, how could an adult? Maybe when she was sad, she unconsciously caught a cold. That can happen. I slipped into her office to look for a note or something written in grease pencil on the schedule board she hung on one side of a filing cabinet. Nothing.

So much for relief.

I went back into the large room. Buster was twitching atop his torn newspaper. I walked over to look at him.

He rose suddenly on his hind legs, holding his two forepaws out together in front of his chest. His whiskers quivered and his beady black eyes stared up at me. Hope springs eternal. I stared back.

He dropped then onto all fours and moved toward the side of his cage. He stood up to put his sharp little claws through the mesh. After a second, I stretched out my fingers very slowly and touched them. He did not withdraw.

What the hell.

Slowly, so as not to alarm him, I pulled open the door to his cage and then, as I had seen nearly every child at the center do, I reached in with both hands cupped and lifted him slowly out.

He didn't struggle. I looked down at him. He felt like a wad of dark wool. His hairless tail was swinging slowly back and forth.

I thought: Come on, Buster, you can't tell me you're happy! Then again, why not? Baines did the same thing with his tail. Even Nigel did once in a while, when he wanted to play.

I took a few careful steps away from the table toward the center of the room and thought for a second about putting him down on the circular rug so he could run free. I didn't. I didn't want anyone to see me playing with him.

Buster seemed totally content. His tail moved a little, and his nose. He looked up at me through the circle of my hands.

I remembered the first time I had ever held a snake. I was in Cub Scouts. I had expected the snake to be slimy and slippery and deathly chill. He hadn't been. What he was was dry and clean and, if not warm, at least not cold.

Suddenly I saw myself: a sensible, medium-sized redheaded twelve-year-old, almost thirteen, standing in the center of a room all alone holding a rat.

I smiled.

Turning a little, I took the few steps back toward Buster's cage and very gently put him down on top of his newspaper. I closed the cage.

Buster huddled a moment without moving. Then he turned

and began snuffling among his wilted lettuce leaves, his shiny claws making little scratching sounds as he nudged and prodded something with his nose.

Frank and I stood in the play yard watching the children. "Well, kid," he said, his hand on my shoulder, his eyes looking without blinking into my own, "this is it."

"This is what?"

"The end." He removed his hand. "Amazing how fast time goes, isn't it?"

"Yeah."

"It's been good having you around, you know? You're good with the kids."

Maybe he didn't know about my nighttime raid at the mission. Maybe no one did.

"Come see us sometime, O.K.?" Frank added then. "As they say in movies, don't be a stranger."

"I won't be. Maybe I'll come back Monday, after school."

Frank smiled thoughtfully. "You'll get busy," he guessed. "People do."

"No, I mean it," I insisted. "I'm not that busy."

Frank patted my shoulder.

"Could you two join us for a minute?"

We both turned to see Ms. Denton pivot back toward the indoors.

Terrific. I wasn't going to get chewed out privately. The whole center was going to hear how I'd messed up.

When we came in from the yard, there was Ms. Denton. I stopped dead, waiting. But she only smiled at me. Wait a minute, I said to myself, half afraid to form my own thought. You don't mean I'm going to get away with it, get out of here without being unmasked as the Midnight Avenger?

Kids flew on all sides, either playing or putting their tiny hands into the larger ones of their parents. In about ten minutes the playroom was empty of "clients."

Debbie and we volunteers stood around sort of awkwardly, not knowing whether we were to leave yet. Ms. Denton stood tall and straight in the center of us all. "There will be a funeral tomorrow," she said at last, looking into the eyes of each of us one by one.

"They've got it figured out?" Frank asked. "I mean, they nabbed whoever it was?"

Ms. Denton shook her head sadly. "Not yet, I'm afraid. There will have to be a complete autopsy. This may not turn out to be a simple case."

Mrs. Mendoza nodded. "So few of these things ever are."

Silently I agreed.

"This is a terrible thing to have happen at any time," Ms. Denton announced, "but coming now, while Benjamin's been with us, to have him see—what? Sometimes the futility, the unpredictability, the…"

"…moments of God's inattention?" Frank suggested.

Ms. Denton shrugged and then smiled, just a little. She reached out for Frank and the two embraced. It was round-robin hug time, like the day before, only this time every hug was individual. Mrs. Mendoza got hers next, then Debbie.

I was the last person Ms. Denton got to. She hugged me and then held me at arm's length. "Doug Bailey said you had something to tell me," she reported. "It isn't about Wendell, is it? I mean, you didn't have a premonition, a sense of the future?"

I shook my head. I was aware that Debbie and Frank and Mrs. Mendoza were getting their coats or sweaters and making ready to leave. I wanted to break Ms. Denton's grip on my shoulders but I felt like my muscles had frozen.

"What is it, Ben?"

"It was about Batista," I said quietly so that no one else could hear. "I found out he wasn't hit."

"Oh, good," Ms. Denton smiled.

I really needed to see that smile just then.

Which, of course, is how I made peace with myself. I hadn't told her a lie. I hadn't told her the complete truth. I hadn't needed to, thanks to Doug Bailey. What I had done was help Ms. Denton find her smile.

"It's been a treat for us, Ben, having you here this week," Ms. Denton told me, stepping away finally. "Working with children doesn't seem very exciting to most people your age."

I resisted my own impulse to tell her it had been plenty exciting for me.

"You're welcome here any time," she added. "Really. I hope you'll stop by from time to time, if only to let us know how you are."

I nodded. "I told Frank I would. On Monday. Maybe I could come by and help a little after school."

"That would be terrific, Ben. I know the children will be happy to see you. We all will."

I nodded and turned away to get my own jacket. I was about to leave Sidewalk's End when Ms. Denton called at me from her office. "You know, Ben, if it's not too personal, I'd love to read your report."

I froze. I had forgotten what was supposed to come next. "O.K. Maybe," I called back after a second.

"Have a wonderful weekend!"

I wondered how wonderful anyone's weekend could be, with pictures of Wendell floating through our dreams.

I opened the front door. It was dark outside and it wasn't until I realized how chill the wind was coming in off the ocean that

I remembered I hadn't a way to get home. I closed the door behind me slowly. That's when I saw Jennie and Teddy Hines waiting for me on the sidewalk beside my bike.

"At last!" Jennie said when I came near them. "It's freezing out here!"

"I brought your bike back," Teddy told me unnecessarily.

"Did you get in trouble?" asked Jennie.

"No," I answered. "After all, I was only doing my job. Anyone would have done the same thing. As a matter of fact, she wants me to come back and work, I'm so good with the kids."

"Are you going to?"

"I might," I told Jennie. "You should come, too. It's probably more fun than working with sick people."

"It wasn't so bad, after a while," Jennie allowed. Then, very quietly, she went on. "But I am glad it's all over."

I looked at Teddy, remembering what he had told me the night before. He understood my look. "I think I can take a break, too. At least for a while."

"Good," I said. "You think your messages got through?"

"What is he talking about?" Jennie wanted to know.

But Teddy didn't answer her. He grinned a little and ducked his head. "I want to think so."

I nodded. Then our situation hit me. I could ride Jennie home on my crossbar, but what about Teddy? He seemed to read my mind. "I better go," he said, leaning the bike into my hand.

Suddenly I thought about telling him my ideas, the ones I'd mentioned to my Dad. I didn't. Dad had said he would come up with something, and I had to trust him. Still, on the very tip of my tongue was what I thought would be good news. But would anyone else? Teddy, and his mother and sister? Aunt Eileen? I couldn't know. Better to wait.

While I was doing all this weighing and measuring in my

mind, Jennie slipped in between us and hitched herself up on the crossbar.

I steadied the bike. I looked at Teddy who was already turning away and starting off into the darkness. "See you Monday!" I called out to him.

His head bobbed. "See you!" he called back.

"Am I too heavy?"

"No way," I told Jennie.

I swung my leg over the bike and put my hands on the bars around her.

"It's uphill," Jennie warned.

I smiled. "Not all the way."

chapter twenty-four

In church the next morning we all stand when the minister asks. We bow our heads. Some people close their eyes, or interlace their fingers prayerfully.

I'm conscious that whatever the feeling is that has been lurking in my mind has moved. Gradually it has sneaked down from my head to my eyes and even lower, to my throat. I swallow hard.

I remember how Teddy had felt cheated by not being able to go to his father's funeral. Suddenly I realize I'm in the same position. In a way, I'm standing there at two services.

Then I hear an amazing sound. Sort of a muffled choking, an "*argh-argh!*", maybe more an "*ack! ack!*" Two shots, just like that–very quick, very close together.

I try to look around without staring. But I don't know where to look. What I'd heard has to be human, but for a moment that's my only clue.

I glance up finally at my dad. His eyes are closed tight, squeezed. His left hand is supporting his right elbow. His right hand is pressed so hard against his mouth that the tips of his fingers are white. His shoulders are shaking silently, and his head shakes back and forth in a "no, no, no."

The feeling I'd feared has jumped from me to him.

I don't move. This isn't something I've ever seen. The minister's voice rises and falls from the front of the church, and soft organ music is being played at the same time.

Dad isn't even trying to control himself.

I peer around us quickly. No one seems to think there is anything strange going on. A few other people are crying, too.

Slowly, so as not to startle him, I lift my right hand. It hangs a moment in midair before lighting ever so gently on Dad's arm.

He doesn't take his hand away from his mouth or open his eyes. His shoulders have folded forward. He's rocking on the balls of his feet. Finally he drops his left arm and puts it across the tops of my shoulders. He pulls me into his side. He squeezes me hard. I can feel his grief ricochet down my body.

I sort of turn into him then.

Life is what Frank had said it was.

Mysterious.